JAMES'S *Joy*

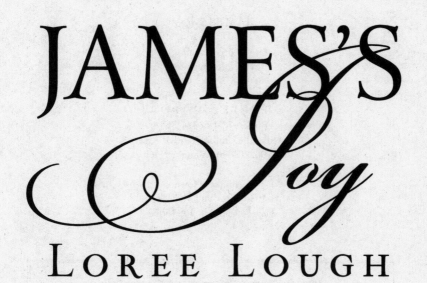

JAMES'S *Joy*

LOREE LOUGH

w

WHITAKER
HOUSE

All Scripture quotations are taken from the King James Version of the Holy Bible.

JAMES'S JOY

Loree Lough
www.loreelough.com

IBSN: 978-1-60374-849-0
eBook: 978-1-60374-850-6
Printed in the United States of America
© 1996, 2013 by Whitaker House

Whitaker House
1030 Hunt Valley Circle
New Kensington, PA 15068
www.whitakerhouse.com

Library of Congress Cataloging-in-Publication Data

Lough, Loree.
    James's joy / Loree Lough.
        pages cm
    ISBN 978-1-60374-849-0 (alk. paper) -- ISBN 978-1-60374-850-6
    I. Title.
    PS3562.O8147J36 2013
    813'.54--dc23

                        2013008303

1 2 3 4 5 6 7 8 9 10 ᴸᴶ 19 18 17 16 15 14 13

PROLOGUE

Freetown, Maryland
February, 1868

James Sheffield stood, gleaming saber in one hand, a half-full bottle of whiskey in the other.

"For pity's sake, Mistah James. Don't go smashin' up what's left of the house," Jeb scolded. Despite James's brutal treatment, the devoted friend and servant refused to leave his side.

The well-muscled body stiffened as he glared at Jeb. "Get out of my way, if you know what's good for you," he snarled.

Jeb gave a sigh of resignation and shook his head. "You need help, Mistah James. You can't go on like this."

"What do you know about going on?" The words were no sooner out of his mouth than James regretted them. He knew full well that in the four years since he returned from the Civil War, bent on burying his memories at the bottom of a bottle, it was Jeb who had kept Plumtree Orchards afloat.

"I know we coulda found some other way to pay off your gamblin' debts," Jeb said angrily. "You didn't have to gamble away Miss

Drewry's hand in marriage. 'Specially not to that good-fer-nothin' Porter Hopkins."

Drewry. His niece, Drewry Sheffield, who was like a daughter to him ever since her parents were killed more than a dozen years earlier. But even his love for Drewry hadn't stopped him from trading her for a sure supply of whiskey. At the reminder of the travesty he'd visited on his only living relative, something snapped in James.

With a roar, he lifted his rapier high, then brought it down, smashing the sideboard mirror. Fragments of glass flew in all directions, then, one by one, rained onto the hardwood floor, each minuscule splinter landing with a delicate tinkle that echoed painfully in his head. He stood there, his sword-arm limp at his side, staring at what had been some of his mother's treasures. They may as well have been the pieces of his broken heart.

Oh, but he was tired. So very tired of his life. If only he could lay down his weapon and his whiskey and start again....

But he deserved no pity—self or otherwise. He became a dastardly being—heartless, cold, bent on destruction. And the evidence, scattered round his feet, shimmered up at him. Fury boiled up from deep within and surged to every nerve ending. With all the strength of his powerful body, James began hacking at the once-elegant mahogany dining room table, where his family talked and laughed and loved. His dead mother's prized lace tablecloth sailed around the room in tatters.

As if possessed, James plunged the saber into the overstuffed chair cushions, sending cotton tufts every which way. Gripped by despair and rage, he kicked the brass ash bucket on the hearth. Clouds of dust billowed up, then floated slowly, slowly down, veiling everything in a filmy layer of gray soot.

Next he smashed the blade into the priceless statuettes on the mantel. Shards of plaster of Paris bounced off the walls and mingled with his curses. He cursed the war. He cursed Porter

Hopkins, who won his plantation during a drunken poker game. He cursed his lovely niece, who ran off rather than marry the old coot in exchange for the deed to Plumtree.

But most of all, James cursed himself...and the bottle that enslaved him more surely than if he sat rotting in a Yankee prison.

⌐

When he at last awoke from his orgy of despair, Jeb was nowhere in sight. Alone again, James raised the whiskey bottle to his lips and, finding it empty, flung it into the fireplace and grabbed another from its hiding place behind the sideboard.

Greedily, he gulped the amber liquid. Its soothing fire spread through his belly. James closed his eyes and sank into the comforting sensation, knowing full well it would vanish as quickly as the morning mists vanished from the orchard.

He listened.

Outside, an early summer storm blew up, and the wind moaned through the magnolias. Its sighing terrified him, for it took him back to the battlefield—his men fallen all around him—groaning in agony as their blood soaked into the Petersburg soil. James heard their cries above his own ragged breaths as he crouched low against the muddy earth...and committed the ultimate act of cowardice.

But there was not enough drink in all the world to drown out the soldiers' mournful wailing. James raised the bottle all the same and drank deeply. Fact was he was a craven coward. Why not prove it to Jeb and Missy and all the world?

His eyes snapped open as he shifted his weight onto his bad leg and felt a sharp pain. *Not sharp enough!* he thought. *No amount of pain can wipe away your guilt. You deserve death—a slow, painful one at that. And after that, hell!*

He felt as if he were perched precariously on a steeply slanting roof, and that in a matter of minutes, he'd slide off the edge and plunge into the darkness, forever. He sold his soul to the Devil with the turn of a card, and he could almost hear the demons laughing.

James stole a furtive glance at his reflection in the cracked mirror above the sideboard. Staring back at him were multiple James Sheffields, with their sweat-matted hair and beards and soot-streaked cheeks. Only the haunted blue of his eyes reminded James of the man he once had been. It was as if he were imprisoned behind that glass—cut off from the world and everyone in it—instead of standing in front of it.

Who could love a face like that? No man or woman he knew, and certainly not God. How could the Almighty care about a drunken fool? Especially when even that fool didn't give a hoot whether he lived or died?

Beads of sweat popped out on his forehead. With a shuddering groan, James tipped back his head and poured the last of the golden heat down his throat.

ONE

Like a sharply honed sword slicing through the tranquil mid-summer afternoon, an anguished scream penetrated the happy chatter of children at play. Only moments before, they were splashing contentedly in the cool, sun-dappled waters of the Gunpowder.

Perched on a smooth boulder, Joy glanced up from her Bible. Every muscle in her neck and shoulders tensed as she scanned the faces of her young charges, in search of the one whose cry of pain or fear foretold certain danger.

Seven, eight, nine, Joy counted silently. She brought ten Suscataway children here to the river's edge to swim on this sultry summer afternoon. Where was the tenth? Then, as if in answer to her unspoken prayer, the piercing wail came again. This time it was more than a scream; the child was calling *her name.*

Immediately, Joy's dark eyes focused on a pair of small bronze arms, churning helplessly as his face appeared, then disappeared, in the froth of river rapids. Realizing that Little Crow was in serious trouble, she stood to her feet, the Good Book toppling from her lap, then froze in horror.

"Help, Joy, help!"

"He's drowning, Joy!"

One hand over her hammering heart, Joy pressed her fingertips against trembling lips. Her first instinct was to run to the water's edge, dive into the river, and swim to Little Crow. But her feet seemed fixed to the spot as she stared helplessly at the boy. He was struggling to remain afloat, submerging repeatedly, then resurfacing only to gurgle out a cry for help and gulp in a breath of air.

Joy's head spun dizzily. She saw the mouths of the children moving to summon her, yet not a word reached her ears. Though it was Little Crow fighting for his life out there, it was a young girl Joy saw in her mind's eye:

"Come out of that water...right thish minute!" Her mother's words, distorted by drink, were thick as cornmeal mush. "Come on now, before you catch your death!"

"But Mama," Joy whimpered, "we're having such fun..." With that, the children who gathered around her lifted Joy, kicking and screaming with glee, and tossed her headfirst into the Gunpowder.

To Ruth, gazing out on the scene through an alcoholic stupor, it appeared that her little daughter was drowning. She leaped into the water and splashed valiantly toward the group of giggling children. "I'll save you! " Ruth called just before she went under. Surfacing, she choked out, "Hang on! I'll save you, child!"

Joy, eyes wide with fright, swam toward her mother. "I'm fine, Mama. It's you who can't swim...."

Ruth tipped back her head and opened her mouth to disagree, only to swallow another mouthful of muddy river water. Coughing and sputtering, she went down for the second time.

"Mama!" Joy wailed. "Mama, swim for the shore!" By now, she was at her mother's side, trying desperately to grab hold of the woman's flailing arms.

But as Ruth continued to struggle, she gradually emerged from her drunken daze. Panic-stricken to find herself in deep water, she clutched at Joy's hair and arms. "Joy, I can't swim! Save me!"

The girl tried with all her might to pull her mother to shore, but the terrified woman proved to be far too strong for the slight twelve-year-old. Ruth, in an attempt to remain afloat, wrapped herself around Joy, as if to buoy herself with her own daughter's body.

Joy went down, once, twice…. On the third dunk, panic seized Joy, also, and instinctively, she pried herself free of her mother's death hold. She'd swim ashore, that's what, and summon help; there were stronger, better swimmers than herself….

Once safe on dry land, the exhausted girl staggered toward the village. Halfway there, something made her turn around. It took just one quick peek over her shoulder to tell her what had happened while she was busy saving her own skin: Her mother had drowned.

If Joy climbed from the water when her mother had asked her to, Ruth wouldn't have misunderstood their harmless antics; she'd never have jumped into the river in the first place.

Joy ran back to the water's edge and stood, helplessly scanning the surface for a sign—any sign—that her mother would reappear. By now all the other children had left the river. Several had run to the village for help, while others stood at Joy's side, whispering to one another what was painfully evident: her mother was dead. And it was all Joy's fault!

A tiny hand, tugging at her own, brought Joy from her reverie. "You have to save him! Save Little Crow, or he'll die!"

Not once since her mother's death had Joy been in the water. Most likely she forgot how to swim. But she had no choice. Praying for guidance, for the strength to do what must be done, she followed the little Indian girl to the bank of the river. This time she had to do it—even if it cost her her own life.

James Sheffield was in no particular hurry to get to town. Drunk, he could almost tolerate Jeb's nagging. But sober, as he was now, the man's good advice drove James to distraction.

"Stop that drinkin', Mistah James," his colored friend said just before he left the house, "'fore you kill yo'self." If he said it once in the past year, Jeb said it a thousand times.

Yes, he promised to give up his whiskey—about as often as Jeb had asked him to give it up. But the heat of the golden elixir was the only warmth in his life these days. How could he part with it? How could Jeb ask him to? Never mind that was the potent brew that caused all his troubles in the first place.

No, that wasn't entirely true. He had to admit that his cowardly actions during the War were the root of his troubles....

An ear-splitting scream broke through the cloying web of self-pity. A child's call for help, followed by the shrieks of several frightened children.

James strained to pinpoint the direction of the shouts, then reined in his horse and maneuvered through the roadside thicket toward the Gunpowder. There, in the clearing, he saw a dozen or so Suscataway Indian children, crying, and pointing toward a boy who was thrashing madly in the water. A lovely young woman, dressed all in white, knelt in the loamy soil at the river's edge. Tears streamed down her face as she opened and closed, opened and closed her fists.

What's she waiting for? James wondered. *The river is deep here; the boy will drown if she doesn't do something, and do it quick!*

Almost at the same moment, he realized that something was wrong. Even from this distance, he recognized the look on her face. It was the paralysis of fear.

Without sparing time for further thought, he leapt from his horse and dove into the cool water, swam to the river's center, grabbed the unconscious boy, and dragged him ashore. Seeing the child safe on dry land again seemed to restore the woman, and she joined James as he knelt beside the boy's limp body.

"How can we thank you?" she whispered. "You're the answer to prayer—a real hero!"

He met her wide, dark eyes, and for an instant, allowed himself to bask in her praise. The instant died quickly. *Hero, indeed*, he scoffed silently. *If only she knew how you earned this limp of yours....*

James turned his attention again to the boy. "We'd best get the water from his lungs. There's not a minute to lose. Here, help me roll him onto his side."

For the next few minutes, the pair worked diligently to revive the water-logged boy. At first, it seemed the child would never catch his breath. But soon, he was sitting up and drying his face with a corner of the blanket. And in no time at all, he was on his feet, receiving the good-natured ribbing of his chums who could now make light of his brush with death.

James, toweling off with another corner of the blanket, took a deep breath. "Mighty close call," he mumbled. "Too close, if you ask me."

The young woman hung her head. "If you hadn't happened along when you did, Little Crow would be..."

He didn't know what possessed him to do it—perhaps the pained expression on her pretty face, or the pitiful little tremor of her voice as it trailed off—but James reached out and took her hand. "Well, now, it's over, isn't it? And the boy will be none the worse for the experience. That's all that counts."

She continued to kneel there, silent and still, slowly shaking her head, her lower lip trembling.

Quickly, before she could begin to cry, James seized the opportunity to introduce himself. With her small hand still engulfed in his, he began lifting and lowering her arm like a pump handle. "Name's Sheffield," he said amiably, "James Sheffield."

When she finally darted a look at him, James's heart throbbed, whether from the purity of her beauty or the raw pain in her round, brown eyes, he didn't know. "And you're…"

"I'm so sorry." She withdrew her hand and stared at the rushing waters of the river. "I—I owe you an explanation…. It is I who should have rescued Little Crow. But since you risked your life, the least I can do is tell you…"

James frowned. "Nonsense. I won't hear another word about it."

She smiled at that—lighting up the shaded bank like a sunburst filtering through the trees. Almost immediately the smile faded. "It's not a terribly long story," she began, getting to her feet. "But I'm afraid it's not a very pretty one, either."

He rose, towering over her. "You don't owe me a thing," he insisted.

"Mr. Sheffield…"

"James," he corrected. "And what do they call you? Lovely Lady?"

She flushed deeply. "My name is Naomi Joy McGuire, but they call me Joy. Pastor McGuire is my father. Perhaps you've heard of him?"

Yes. James had heard of Sam McGuire, the minister who took over at St. Johns while James had been off…fighting…in the Civil War. *Fighting, ha!*

"You see," she went on. "I have an intense aversion to water…. It started the day my mother drowned."

Joy told her story quickly and without embellishment, yet sparing none of the details. James watched with fascination as first pain, then guilt, then sorrow crossed her pretty features.

"It was my fault…all my fault," she concluded, slumping against the trunk of a nearby tree. "If I hadn't…"

"I've never heard anything more ridiculous in all my life," he growled. "It was the drink that killed your mother, not you!

Whiskey is a powerful foe; once you're under its spell, rational thought is impossible." *And who ought to know that better than you, James Sheffield!*

For the first time since returning from the War, Jeb's words made complete sense: "You ain't jus' hurtin' yo'self, Mistah James. You is hurtin' all of us what loves and cares 'bout you...."

Joy told James she came away from her mother's struggle with an ugly gash on her cheek. In time, the wound healed. But he sensed that Joy bore a deeper scar that would take much longer to heal. That she carried such a heavy burden all these years touched him in the deepest part of his heart.

"You can't talk sense to a drunkard," he added more gently. "You tried to save her, but the whiskey talked louder than you did. You didn't kill your mother, Joy. Liquor killed her."

There were tears in her big eyes when she said softly, "Thank you, James. You're a very kind and understanding man."

I understand far more than you know, thought James miserably. *And what would you think of me if you learned why I'm so knowledgeable on the subject of drink!* Why, she'd turn and run like a scared rabbit. He blinked the thought away.

He was on his way to town, he recalled now, to replenish his own liquor supply, or they'd never have met at all. *Maybe,* James thought, *it's a sign from heaven that you should take Jeb's advice and spend your energies on the farm instead of the booze.*

⌒

Joy thought about the intriguing man all the way back to the Suscataway village...and as she walked from the village to the cottage she shared with her father...and as she prepared her simple supper...and while she cleaned up the dishes.

Joy thought of James later, too, as she sat rocking in the parlor, darning her father's socks. When Samuel returned from his church business in Philadelphia, he'd find every sock mended!

Right up until the moment she drifted off to sleep, James Sheffield's ruggedly handsome face hovered in her memory.

He cut quite a dashing figure, she decided, despite the thick, angry scar that twisted along his right cheek, despite whatever brutal injury caused his limp. His clear eyes were exactly the color of the summer sky as he knelt beside her on the riverbank, his dark hair and beard glistening with silvery droplets as he pumped river water from Little Crow's lungs.

But those massive shoulders bore a burden of considerable weight, this much she knew. For though she told him in minute detail about the events surrounding her mother's death, James had very carefully and deliberately avoided revealing a single fact about his own life. She told him, too, of her faith in God, without whom she would not have survived the tragedy. James admitted he never had much faith, adding that he envied hers.....

Strange. Just last week, she overheard her father and his assistant, Matthew Frost, discussing James Sheffield. Their comments were far from complimentary. It was well known that James was the town drunk, a ruthless gambler, and a womanizer. Even Joy heard the rumors. But after the episode in the river, she had a different opinion of him—courageous rescuer, kind and compassionate...friend.

James Sheffield hadn't set foot in a church in years, her father said, and his bad habits were slowly destroying what had once been the most productive fruit orchard in northern Maryland. But how could such things be true? Joy wondered. Could a reprobate who returned from the War bruised and broken inside and out have risked his life to save a child? Could a man who preferred whiskey and poker and wild women to the godly life have listened so intently to her sorrowful story, then offered such tender words of consolation?

Joy doubted it. She preferred to believe that what she saw in those crisp blue eyes—honesty, integrity, strength of character—was the real James Sheffield, though perhaps buried deep within. If she was right, maybe he could become once again the man he was before the War....

At least, Joy sincerely hoped so.

TWO

"Not a penny more. Take it or leave it." Duncan Green wiped his hands on his dirty apron and peered at James over spectacles that perched on the bridge of his bulbous nose.

Humiliated at having to barter his mother's silver tea service, piece by piece, with the owner of the general store, James's cheeks flushed crimson. Thinning his lips, he stared at the light reflecting from the top of Green's bald head. "You can surely do better than that," he bit out. "This teapot's been in the Sheffield family for generations." James thumped it onto the counter. "Take a gander at the hallmark!" he demanded. "The piece came all the way from England with my grandmother."

Green squinted as he inspected the inscription stamped onto the bottom of the teapot while James drummed his fingers impatiently on the marred wooden countertop. If the oily shopkeeper took much longer deciding, he'd win the bartering game—again.

James licked his parched lips. He hadn't had a drink all day. He planned to remedy that soon. But only after purchasing the food on Missy's list and enough soap to make another batch of the home-brewed insect repellent he planned to drizzle over the saplings Jeb planted earlier in the week. He flexed his muscles, feeling an unaccustomed twinge in his right shoulder. He hadn't done any real work since the War. But something in Joy McGuire's guileless face when she called him a "hero" for rescuing that little Indian boy, had pricked his conscience. And much to Jeb's surprise—and his own—he was getting up at first light to pick sleeping beetles from the Mackintosh trees!

"Thirty dollars. Not a penny more."

Green's offer roused James from his daydream. He stretched to his full six-foot-two-inch height and squared his shoulders. "It's worth twice that, Green, and you know it."

The storekeeper shrugged and handed the swan-necked pot back to James. "That's my final offer." The flinty eyes narrowed. "I'm the only show in town, and you know it."

Just then a gentle, lilting voice floated over James's shoulder. "Why, Mr. Green, you should be ashamed! I would have never thought you capable of cheating a man on the fair value of an item."

James spun around in time to meet the sparkling brown eyes of Joy McGuire. Sunlight, filtering through the windows, glinted from her long, ebony hair and cast an angelic aureole about her head. He returned her friendly smile. Of all the people he preferred not know about his desperate attempt to resupply his liquor cabinet, it was this lovely woman. James couldn't help but wish that Green's grimy floorboards would open up and swallow him.

Joy stepped past him and leaned over the counter.

She ran a slender fingertip along the pot's long, silver spout. "Just last week, I saw a teapot very like this one in Baltimore." She raised her delicate chin and met Green's eyes with a challenge. "Can you believe it fetched fifty dollars?"

Mouth agape, the storekeeper folded his arms over his chest and shook his head in resignation. James knew that as an occasional churchgoer, the owner of the general store wouldn't want to look bad in the eyes of the pastor's daughter. "You're right, of course, Miss Joy." Then, facing James, he cleared his throat. "Fifty dollars, Sheffield. Take it or leave it."

"Done!" James agreed, flashing Joy a grateful grin.

⌒

Outside the store, James sat on a bench and counted his money. If he waited until Miss McGuire finished her business with Green, maybe James could persuade her to sit with him long enough to thank her properly for coming to his assistance.

Still, if his reputation preceded him, she'd likely be reluctant to be seen in public with the town drunk. Thanking him for saving Little Crow on the riverbank the other day was one thing; keeping company with him for all the town to see was quite another.

When she emerged from the store, he sat up straight and held his breath. Would she walk past and merely nod politely? Or would she—

"How nice to see you again so soon, Mr. Sheffield." Her warm greeting answered his unspoken question. "James," he reminded her.

Without waiting for an invitation, Joy nodded and sat down beside him.

"Thanks for helping me out in there." James scanned her face for any sign of revulsion over his bartering...over being this near him...over the stench of whiskey that no doubt emanated from his every pore. Seeing none, he breathed a silent sigh of relief.

She settled her packages beside her, then rested her hand on his sleeve. "But James, it's the least I could do, after what you did for Little Crow...."

James shrugged off her gratitude. "I'm just glad I happened to be in the neighborhood at the time."

She patted his arm again. "The children and I have been praying for you ever since."

He couldn't help but notice the intriguing dimples that danced in her cheeks when she smiled, the genuine warmth that glowed in her dark eyes. "I wouldn't waste too many prayers on me if I were you."

Her lovely smile vanished like smoke, leaving a disapproving frown. "Now, why on earth would you say such a thing!"

He was sitting sideways on the bench so he could face her head-on, but in response to Joy's point-blank question, James faced forward and crossed his arms over his chest. "I don't believe in the goodness of God. At least, I don't believe it exists for the likes of me."

She didn't respond immediately, and the long moment of silence stretched out unbearably. Would she choose this time to stand, gather her packages, and walk away? Would she tell him he was right—that God had no time for the likes of James Sheffield? Not that he blamed her if she did....

Her soft voice penetrated his fog of self-pity. "None of us deserves God's mercy, James. Every last one of us is a sinner." She leaned forward slightly to peer into his eyes. "But if we choose to accept it, we're forgiven sinners...beloved sinners."

He ran a hand through his hair, over his unkempt beard, suddenly wishing he spruced up a bit before coming to town. But then he hadn't expected to be entertaining such a beauty. James shifted uneasily on the hard bench, wondering if he'd ever live long enough to have a faith like hers.

Beloved sinners, he mused. "That may be true for others," he began, making eye contact at last, "but after the life I've led..."

Without warning, Joy grabbed his hand. "I have an idea! Why don't you come to church with me on Sunday?"

Was he hearing things? Was she really asking him to go to church with her? *Him...a* cowardly, drunken bum? He stared deep into the dark pools of her eyes. *A man could get lost in there.*

She gave his hand a little squeeze that sent shivers up his spine.

"Well?" Joy persisted. "What do you say? Will you come to church this next Sunday?"

For an instant, James forgot about his slovenly appearance, forgot that he earned his reputation as the town drunk, forgot what a coward he was, forgot even that she just witnessed his blatant need for whiskey, even forgot his thirst for the stuff. In fact, no one was more surprised than James when he smiled and said, "I'd love to go to church with you."

Five hours later, James leaned his elbows on a saloon table and bet Porter Hopkins his last two dollars.

The red-faced drunk let out a bellow. "Why, Sheffield, don't you know to quit when you're ahead?" He laid his cards on the table, fanning them so James could see the straight flush.

But the golden glow of drink set in, and instead of punching Hopkins, as he might have done after losing such a slug of money, James laughed loudly, slapped his thigh, and slung his arm around the bare-shouldered barmaid beside him.

Kitty plucked a purple feather from her headdress and tickled his nose. In the stifling heat, perspiration caused her rouge to run, but in James's inebriated state, the whole world looked smeary.

He and Kitty stumbled out of the saloon and into the velvety black night. Her voice was a loud whine, complaining that she couldn't believe he lost all his money already. The drunken pair weaved along the wooden walkway, heading for James's horse, still tethered where his master left him hours earlier.

As they staggered past the undertaker's establishment, James burst into a slurred rendition of "Goober Peas," the wartime ballad celebrating the lowly peanut. "Peas, peas, peas, peas, eating goober peas," he roared.

"Goodness how delicious," Kitty chimed in, "eating goober peas!"

So energetic was their song that James didn't notice the tiny woman hurrying along the boardwalk until he sideswiped her with his elbow as he hoisted a salute to goober peas.

The woman stumbled from the boardwalk, her blue gingham dress tangling around her ankles, the contents of her sewing basket flying in all directions. She landed, face down, in the street.

At the commotion, James squinted and grabbed the railing for support, trying to focus his blurred vision. "Sorry, ma'am," he sputtered.

Only when she turned to accept his outstretched hand did he recognize his victim. It was Joy McGuire he just knocked into the mud!

⁓

Joy dipped hot water from the caldron above the fire into the washbasin. The mud stains would probably never come out of her best dress, she realized, though she soaked the soiled area in Borax and Fuller's earth. She even tried lye, but the ugly spots refused to yield.

But it wasn't the ruined dress that caused her tears.

What they say about him is true, she moaned inwardly. *Now I've seen it with my own eyes! He's a drunk!*

Sadly, Joy shook her head as she rubbed the blue and white fabric against the washboard's silvery ribs. She saw many Suscataway braves succumb to the temptation of whiskey—a temptation for which there was no cure but total abstinence.

Could James Sheffield take the cure? she wondered.

The townspeople whispered behind his back, but there was more to him than what could be seen on the surface. Joy knew it as surely as she knew there was a God.

She heard it said that, before James went off to war, he opened his home to his orphaned niece. That he operated Plumtree Orchards at a tidy profit and donated money to the church in his deceased parents' names. But all that happened before she and her father came back to town six years ago.

Still, she witnessed James's courage at the riverbank, witnessed, too, his gentlemanly manners at the general store earlier that day. She supposed it was divine intervention that forced her to see the ugly side of handsome James Sheffield.

All her life, Joy refused to be less than honest with herself. She had to admit that she found his masculinity attractive, very attractive. She wanted to believe, too, that integrity and strength of character lived within him—a strength of character that, when pushed to the proving point, as it was on the Gunpowder's banks—would leave the town gossips with no fodder for their speculation.

And to be brutally honest, Joy knew that if James didn't reform, it was only a matter of time before whiskey claimed him in an ignoble death, as it claimed so many of the Suscataway braves. She allowed herself to envision the beginnings of a friendship growing between her and the handsome hero. But there could be no deepening of the relationship if he continued to allow alcohol to enslave him.

Still scrubbing at the stain, Joy recalled the despair in James's voice when he spoke of God. She sensed his loneliness, saw, too, the pain this absence of faith painted on his haggard face.

Straightening from her work over the washbasin, Joy knew what she must do. If she didn't at least try to help James find comfort in the faith of her friend, she wasn't worthy of His calling. Somehow, with God's help, she'd bring James the Good News that he wasn't alone. She'd help him understand that God would be his friend, too, and would be like a sister who'd help him battle his demons.

Joy squeezed the wash water from her dress with all the strength she could muster; she had to try!

THREE

Every footfall echoed loudly through the big, empty house as James limped from room to room. It seemed that with each reverberating step, he was again reminded of his solitary status. He had no one…not friend nor brother, not parent nor lover to help quiet the sound of his loneliness.

Holding the half-empty bottle of whiskey at arm's length, he moaned, "You're all I've got in the world."

After taking a long, slow swallow of the stinging liquid, James began the climb up the curved mahogany staircase. It was as if each tread mocked him as he made his way to the second floor of the mansion: *Alone, alone, alone!*

He locked himself in his room, as he did hundreds of times before, then threw open the French doors that led to his balcony. The wind, hot and dry, tousled the dark waves of his hair. With one hand, he held the neck of the bottle tight against him; with the other, he steadied himself against the railing. At his touch bright white paint chips loosened and rained upon the worn floorboards.

Staggering, he took a step away from the railing. Frowning drunkenly, he stared down at the flakes, then at the handrail. Such a small thing, really, and yet its disrepair loomed large in his mind, for the railing that surrounded his balcony was symbolic of everything about his life.

With his thumbnail, he absently picked at another loose chip. Holding it between his thumb and forefinger, James watched it slowly disintegrate, as if his touch alone were enough to destroy.

James took another long swig of the whiskey, rolled the prickling potion around in his mouth, then swallowed, and waited for the burning sensation that would follow when it hit bottom. He closed his eyes and sighed when he felt the sting, then waited for the familiar dizzying heat to dull his headache.

He waited ten seconds. Twenty. A full minute. Nothing. James downed another gulp. Surely this would bring the relief he craved.

But it did not.

Was he really so far gone that two full bottles of whiskey could no longer make him forget all that he had become? He held the bottle out once more, tipped it right, then left. The nostrum glittered like liquid gold in the bright sunlight, casting shards of brilliant, reflected beams upon the toes of his leather boots and the once-gleaming white floorboards beneath them.

The translucent beams reminded him of Joy: pure, clear light sparkled in her eyes, too. Or at least, until last night....

How could he have forgotten he was to meet her at the church? How could he have allowed Porter Hopkins' brusque invitation to thrust all thought of Joy from his mind?

It hadn't taken long to get roaring drunk, to spend the last of the coins in his pocket, to find a willing barfly to cling to his arm. Together, he and Kitty found their way down the middle of Main Street, laughing and singing at the top of their lungs.

Not until she lay in a graceless heap in the mud at his feet did James realize he knocked Joy down. He was so drunk, he hadn't even realized she was anywhere near!

At first, she appeared puzzled, apparently failing to realize that he was drunk. In that brief, fleeting instant, she smiled as if glad to see him. But in the next interminably long moment, as his condition registered in her quick mind, revulsion and fear widened her lovely eyes.

Without a word, she scrambled to her feet, gathered up her sewing materials, and hurried away. Her final perusal of him lasted but the blink of an eye, yet during that tiny tick in time, Joy's quiet disappointment rang louder than his drunken floozy's garish laughter.

And before he could summon the presence of mind to attempt apology or explanation, she was gone, without a word or backward glance. Even in his inebriated state, James knew he saw that look of disgust every time he closed his eyes.

Now, as he teetered drunkenly on the neglected balcony, he saw it again. Her open, trusting expression closed at the sight of him—drunk and disorderly—like a steel gate. The fact that she didn't approve rankled. But why should he care? He knew her only a short time. Unaccountably, however, her opinion mattered. It mattered very much.

There was but one way to win her approval. James took another long, hard look at the whiskey bottle. His mouth watered for a taste of it. He licked his lips and swallowed in anticipation. Yes... he wanted to earn back Joy's respect.

But did he want it enough to give up the golden elixir?

⌒

She couldn't get the image of him, staggering and swaggering, out of her mind. *So*, Joy said to herself, *what they've been saying in town is true, after all. James Sheffield is a no-good drunkard.*

The thought haunted Joy long into the dark, lonely night.

At first, she chastised herself for judging the man so harshly. Perhaps drunkenness wasn't a way of life with him, after all, but rather a momentary backslide. He hadn't been the least bit out of order that day on the riverbank, when he risked his own life to save Little Crow's.

But Joy knew enough about the demon, alcohol, to know that even the most tormented of souls could pretend normalcy—for short periods of time. More than likely, she and Little Crow simply had the good fortune to meet up with James during one of his more sober moments. Hadn't he said much the same, sitting on the bench outside the general store?

Joy squared her shoulders and lifted her chin in determination. She would not deliberately avoid James Sheffield, but neither would she seek him out. If another meeting between them took place in the near future, she'd be cordial. Polite. Nothing more, nothing less was required of a good Christian.

Or was it?

⌣

It was the first time Joy wore the full-circle black skirt she fashioned from the bolt of cotton her father brought back from his last trip to Philadelphia. She especially liked the fashionably wide waistband and the broad ruffle at the hem. This morning, she chose a white organza blouse with balloon sleeves to wear with it. After plaiting her hair in a single, thick braid, Joy tied it with a black satin bow, then fastened a matching bow at the high collar of her blouse.

"You look lovely today, Joy," Matthew said when she entered the tiny space her father called his office. "But then, that's nothing new."

Joy flushed with embarrassment at this unexpected compliment. She knew Matthew nearly four years, ever since the handsome young minister arrived from Boston to assist her father in running St. John's. He was pleasant enough, in his stern-yet-deferential way. But he never showed such an active interest in her...until lately.... Joy wondered what caused the noticeable transformation.

"Where are you off to so early in the morning?" he wanted to know.

His smile seemed out of place. Joy wished for a nice way to tell him he ought to display it more often, for it softened the hard angles and planes of his face and gave him a more youthful, innocent look. "I'm headed for the Suscataway village," she said. "The children are all the way up to the sevens on their multiplication tables."

Matthew nodded patronizingly. "You're doing remarkable work there, Joy. Before you took them on, those people were uneducated, illiterate barbarians."

His smug, holier-than-thou attitude toward the Indians always annoyed her. "They couldn't read or write, I'll give you that," she said, a tremor of anger ringing in her voice, "but they were never barbarians." Shouldn't she know? Her own mother was one of them! But then Matthew probably didn't know that. Her father rarely spoke of Ruth anymore...probably thought the subject of Joy's mother would only bring more pain.

Matthew's smile vanished, replaced by his now-familiar scowl. He sat at her father's desk and began leafing through a stack of papers.

"Why don't you come with me, Matthew? I'm sure they'd be pleased to have you. You have so much to share...."

He looked up abruptly. "Me? Why, what on earth could I possibly share with those people?"

Matthew spoke as if the Suscataways were not human, but some alien form of life he was forced to endure. "They might like to learn something of the New Testament," she suggested, "and you've always got your nose buried in Luke or Mark or..."

Matthew grunted. "Now, that's a bit of a stretch, even for a dreamer like you, isn't it?"

Joy gasped, her eyes wide with disbelief. "Are you saying the Suscataways are not smart enough to understand God's Word… or not worthy to hear it?"

He shrugged indifferently. "What's the difference?"

How can he call himself a man of God? Joy fumed. "The Lord loves everyone equally, and every single person has a right to hear His Word!" she reminded him.

He shrugged again and turned his attention to the paperwork on his desk. "If you'll excuse me, I have a lot to do." He waved his hand, dismissing her like some errant child.

With a huff, she whirled around and stormed from her father's office, almost forgetting why she went there in the first place. And if she hadn't needed the arithmetic book for the day's lesson, she wouldn't have returned at all.

Joy blew back into the room, stomped over to the bookshelf, grabbed the book, and without so much as looking at Matthew, tucked it under her arm and marched from the room. *I'll say a prayer for your mortal soul, Matthew Frost,* she promised, *so that your superior attitude won't trip you as you make your way through the Golden Gate!*

On the way to the village, Joy pondered what had just taken place. Too many Christians were like Matthew, she supposed, feeling that they had somehow earned God's love by their own actions. But it didn't give them the right to judge lost sheep as a lost cause! In fact, quite the contrary. It was Christians whom God was trusting to reach out to unbelievers. *And how can we do that, if we walk around feeling better than everyone else?*

So lost in thought was she that Joy didn't notice the hulking shadow that crossed her path, didn't hear the halting footsteps of the man who approached. "Joy," he said, startling her so badly that she dropped the huge arithmetic book, "I must speak with you."

Joy looked up into the haunted face of James Sheffield. Instantly, she tensed as he picked up her book and held it out to her. "I—I'm afraid I haven't time just now. I'm on my way to the village—to give the children a multiplication quiz," she rambled.

James smiled gently before putting the book in her hands. "It won't take but a moment," he promised. "Perhaps if I walk along with you, we can accomplish two things at once."

In answer to her puzzled frown, he held up one finger. "First, I won't prevent you from arriving on time for the lesson, and," he added, waggling a second finger. "I can apologize for my abominable behavior yesterday."

Joy bristled. "I'm sure I don't know what you're talking about!" She picked up speed and hurried off in the direction of the village.

She went a good twenty paces before realizing that she could not hear the sound of his footsteps in pursuit. She lagged a bit, but she would not give him the satisfaction of turning around to see if he headed back toward town or was still standing in the middle of the street where she left him.

But before she could give in to her inclination, James fell into step beside her. "No doubt you've heard all about me," he said without hesitation. "I hoped to show you only my best side; I'm sorrier than you'll ever know that now you've seen firsthand what a lout I really am."

A furrow creased Joy's smooth brow as she met his gaze. "Why should you care what I think?"

It was a fair question, after all. James searched her face for the suggestion of superiority that usually accompanied any reference to his "condition." It relieved him greatly to see no trace of it there, and he smiled. He honestly didn't know why her opinion of him mattered so much.

Shrugging, he attempted to answer her question. "Perhaps you came along just when I began to wonder what I've become…and why." Stuffing both hands into the pockets of his trousers, James shook his head. "Or perhaps it's simply that I'm a bit...smitten."

Joy clutched the book to her bosom in an attempt to still the wild fluttering of her heart. *Smitten*, did he say? *Smitten with me?* She considered telling him she'd sooner jump headfirst into the Gunpowder than acknowledge such a thing. Why, it bordered on insulting to admit that someone like James Sheffield—gambler, alcoholic, womanizer—was smitten with her.

Suddenly, she heard a familiar all-knowing tone in her own thoughts. *Why, Joy McGuire*, she scolded herself, *you're no better than Matthew Frost!*

She was walking quickly, so quickly that her lame companion was having a difficult time keeping up. Deliberately slowing her pace, she turned to him, an inspiration occurring to her. "Come with me," she said, her voice strong and sure as the idea took hold. His dark brows rose in confusion. "Now? Me? But what...why...?

Joy grabbed his hand. "You'll see," she said, tugging him along the path. "You'll see."

⌒

James had been home for hours, but nothing he did—pacing the floor, rearranging the books on his shelf, gazing out over the groves of fruit trees—could distract him from what he saw on the periphery of the Suscataway village.

From the moment Joy introduced him to Red Shirt, James didn't know which startled him more—what he saw there or the striking similarity to his own miserable existence.

Soon after they met, Red Shirt freely admitted that he, too, was once under the dominion of the demon alcohol. As the two men strolled past the birch-hewn palisade that surrounded the village, Red Shirt explained who lived in the various wigwams. The largest hut, constructed of bent saplings and bulrushes, belonged to his father, Chief Gray Hawk. Red Shirt, Gray Hawk's only son, resided in the slightly smaller, adjacent but with his wife, Running Deer, and their son, Little Crow.

More than once, as they made their way through the maze of abodes and storage facilities, Red Shirt thanked James for saving Little Crow's life. Time and again, feeling more and more uncomfortable, James insisted no thanks were necessary.

By the time they reached the outer limits of the village, James felt he made a friend, though he wasn't able to analyze the relationship. There was a common bond, of course, in their dependence upon whiskey. But they were not alone in their enchantment with the stuff, James was soon to learn.

"This," said Red Shirt, his gesture encompassing the area surrounding them, "is the home of the men who have succumbed to the Great Liar."

James surveyed the ramshackle huts that stood in sharp contrast to the tidy rows of wigwams in the village proper. Men of every age and size staggered or shuffled about, lost in a drunken stupor.

James swallowed hard. He heard that some religions practiced shunning their own as a sign of their disgrace. Banishment, he believed, was the strictest, cruelest form of punishment. "They're outcasts?"

Red Shirt nodded sadly. "Not so long ago, I walked among them. If not for Joy McGuire..." His voice caught in his throat, and the proud Indian stood taller, squared his chin to regain his composure. "Those who refuse to obey the rules set forth to protect us all cannot be allowed to live among us."

James frowned. "But why? It's the alcohol that fogs their brains, makes them do the wretched things they do. It's not their fault...."

Red Shirt held up a silencing hand. "That, my new friend, is whiskey's biggest lie." After a long moment of silence, the Indian continued, "This is your future, my friend. Look hard at it, and ask yourself if you can live this life until God calls you home."

As his thoughts swirled, James paced the length and breadth of the terrace, considering Red Shirt's challenge. Was he destined to live as the once-proud braves lived now, shunned by friends and family, feared by their own offspring? In truth, it was not much worse than the life he now lived—a bleak and forlorn existence, to be sure.

Before the War, James loved life, people, was a genial host, opening Plumtree to friends and family on festive occasions. How long had it been? How much longer could he go on living this half-life?

Sunlight, slanting off the bottle of whiskey on the table just inside the terrace doors, now caught his eye, stirring him from his thoughts. "Come to me," it beckoned. "Drown your sorrows in my soothing promises."

His taste buds tingled, yearning for a sip of mind-numbing brew. But what had Red Shirt said? "It's whiskey's big lie..."

James forced himself to look elsewhere. His gaze settled on the gnarled little trees that should, at this time of year, be burdened with ripening fruit. Instead, their yellowing leaves told of neglect that robbed them of their ability to produce.

One barn door hung askew on rusting iron hinges, catching the summer breeze and banging relentlessly against its support wall.

The split-rail fence surrounding the barnyard echoed James's abandonment. Plumtree Orchards, like James himself, was in danger of complete and utter decay. Did he have time to right years of wrongs?

"Mistah James..."

Jeb's deep voice broke his momentary trance. He turned to the man who, for decades, refused to leave his side. Suddenly, exhaustion enveloped him and James dropped wearily onto the stone bench at the edge of the flagstone terrace and buried his face in his hands. "What is it, Jeb?"

"Has you been drinkin' agin, Mistah James?"

James sighed. "No." He caught a glimpse of the temptress from the corner of his eye as he glanced up at the faithful servant. "At least, not yet."

"I got no money to buy feed for the animals," Jeb said. "What you want me to sell this time?"

James rubbed his tired, bloodshot eyes. When was the last time he had a complete, uninterrupted, non-whiskey-induced night's sleep? He stood, limped slowly into the house, and surveyed what remained of the once-elegant furnishings that were his mother's pride and joy. The player piano, nestled snug against the parlor wall, captured his attention. It would bring a hundred dollars, at least. "Sell the piano," James said dully.

Jeb's sharp intake of air made James wince. "But Mistah James. The pi-anny was yo' mama's fav'rite thing in this whole house."

And so it was. He remembered how she sat for hours, plunking the ivory keys, humming some favorite hymn. James shrugged. His mother had been gone for years now. What good was the old thing anyway, save to serve as a dust-catcher? No one had touched the keys since…since Drewry ran away.

Suddenly, the instrument took on new meaning, as the bridge between him and his beloved missing niece. "All right. The piano stays."

Facing Jeb, he ran both hands through his hair. "It doesn't matter what you sell. Sell every stick of furniture that's left, for all I care…but leave my mother's piano."

FOUR

James walked his horse to the livery stable and tossed a coin into the attendant's outstretched hand. "Give him a good brushing," James instructed, "and see that he gets a long drink of cool water."

Winded and sweaty after the twenty-mile ride from Plumtree to Freetown, the stallion snorted his appreciation for the well-earned respite. The animal carried his burden well; now it was time for James to carry his own. And it would take more than a mere coin, pressed into the hand of a stable boy, to relieve him of that responsibility.

James headed in the direction of the general store, the silver tray tucked under his arm. If he believed in prayer, he'd have sent a silent petition heavenward that Joy McGuire wouldn't see him barter away yet another piece of his mother's tea service.

He glanced up and down the street, checking to make sure she was nowhere about. But the only person in view was Matthew Frost, St. John's serious-minded assistant pastor. Frost arrived in Freetown shortly after James left to fight in the Civil War and, because James could count on one hand the number of times he attended services since returning from the battlefield, the two men had only a nodding acquaintance. So it was a surprise to James when the man stopped in front of him.

"Brother James, I must speak with you about a matter of conscience and godly propriety."

Matthew's condescending tone grated on James's nerves, and he made no attempt to hide his annoyance. "What is it?" he ground out without missing a step on his way to the general store.

Matthew cleared his throat, then nodded toward the church. "Perhaps we could step into my office. What I have to say involves one of our good sisters, Joy McGuire."

James halted in his tracks and turned to face the young pastor, whose self-righteous expression only further incensed James.

"Brother, I'm well aware that before my tenure, you were most generous in your support of the church, prior to…shall we say… your regrettable 'lapse' in the faith."

James grimaced. "Just spit it out, Frost," he said through clenched teeth.

Matthew blinked several times and licked his lips. After taking a deep breath, he squared his shoulders. "I must insist that you show some respect for Miss McGuire's reputation in this town."

James narrowed his gaze as his fist doubled instinctively. Pressing the silver tray tighter against his chest, he summoned the control to resist punching the assistant pastor in the jaw.

"The other day," Matthew continued, pointing toward the bench outside the general store, "you invited Miss McGuire to sit there, in full view of the whole community!" Matthew shook his head solemnly. "Brother, you must realize what consorting with a man like you can do to the reputation of a lady like Miss McGuire…particularly considering the fact that she already faces certain biases concerning…uh, her half-breed heritage, a matter I've only recently come to understand."

James drew back his free hand, but caught himself short. He took a step closer and leaned into Matthew. "What's her heritage got to do with me?"

Matthew cleared his throat again, then tugged at both sleeves of his somber black coat. Fear constricted the pupils of his green eyes, but he stood his ground. "Why, I'm referring to your regrettable relationships with alcohol, gambling, and the loose ladies of The Silver Dollar Saloon, of course."

James pocketed the threatening fist. "I have too much respect for Miss McGuire," he began, dropping his voice to a menacing growl, "to be anything but a complete gentleman in her company." Though he wasn't wearing a tie himself, James ran a finger around the neckline of his collarless shirt, remembering the night when, in a drunken fog, he knocked her into the mud. Bristling, he added, "Furthermore, I have too much respect for her to refer to her as a 'half-breed.'"

The barely suppressed fury in James's tone caused Matthew to back up a step. "Perhaps my words are harsh, Brother James, but the truth often stings. Miss McGuire has had enough to overcome in her short life without being seen in the company of the town drunk."

In his pocket James's fist opened, closed, opened again. "Exactly what makes you the guardian of Miss McGuire's virtue?"

Matthew proudly poked out his chin. "I, Brother James, am the young lady's intended." With a self-satisfied smirk, the pastor tapped a fingertip against the brim of his black hat, and walked away.

James stood there in stunned silence. Matthew Frost...Joy's future husband? How could James have been so thick-skulled as to hope she saw him as more than a friend, when all along she was promised to another?

About five feet down the boardwalk, Matthew hesitated and turned to call back to James. "I hear-tell whiskey's in short supply down at the Silver Dollar today," he said, all traces of refinement absent from his practiced voice.

James closed the gap between them in two long strides until they were standing a shoulder's width apart. He made no reply, but merely stood there, glaring into Matthew's face.

But the pastor wasn't that easily intimidated. "You were on your way to the saloon, weren't you?" he taunted.

The silver tray under his arm betrayed James, and sheepishly, he ducked his head, reminded of his real purpose in town. His plan was a simple one—to trade the tray for folding money, which he'd unfold at the Silver Dollar.

Without a word, James turned on his heel and headed for the general store, both men knowing full well that Matthew's question needed no answer.

James was sober for the first time in days.

Despite his roaring headache, he was thinking clearly—clearly enough to know that the anger bubbling in the pit of his stomach wasn't really aimed at the arrogant young pastor, Matthew Frost. James's rage had only one target—himself.

He hadn't gone to the Silver Dollar after doing his business with Green at the general store, after all. Instead, he'd walked to the north edge of town and stood on the bank of the Gunpowder River. A crow flew overhead, its lonely, echoing cry calling up every anguished emotion in James. The tray had brought a good price, and the thirty dollars, tucked into his shirt pocket, crinkled against his vest. James pressed it to him and closed his eyes.

The money would buy enough whiskey to see him through this day, and many more. Running his tongue over his dry, parched lips, James yearned for a swallow of the bitter brew. Sighing deeply, he forced himself to focus on Matthew's parting words: "You were on your way to the saloon, weren't you?"

The currency, warm now beneath his palm, seemed to whisper to him. *That's right. Use me*, it said. *Take me to the Silver Dollar and trade me for a few hours of oblivion....*

You are what you are, he told himself in disgust. *No sense fighting it. And even if you tried, you haven't the strength to whip this beast.*

Just then, a fish broke the surface of the water, its silvery scales flashing as it leaped high into the air, then spiraled downward again. It was about there—at the center—where Little Crow would have surely drowned if James did not come to the rescue.

Deep within began a sorrowful litany: *You saved a child, but you can't save yourself.* He laughed mirthlessly, the sound echoing back from the far shore of the Gunpowder. *You can't save yourself?*

Could he? Was it possible?

On the spot, James made a decision. He would, at least, try. With a determined spring in his step, he headed for the livery to collect his horse. He'd race back to Plumtree, before he succumbed to the temptation to stop at the Silver Dollar and spend the money he traded for his mother's silver tray.

All the way home, James repeated his newly made resolution: *I will try to loose Whiskey's hold over me.... I will try to loose Whiskey's hold over me....*

Now, sitting alone in his wrecked dining room, itching for a drink, James tried to sort out his thoughts. Surprisingly, the thing that nagged at him most was not Frost's patronizing attitude, but the fact that he declared his intentions to wed Joy McGuire.

James didn't want to believe it. There must be some mistake. How could she have committed herself to that pompous, self-righteous prude? Matthew Frost was not worthy of her.

Besides, James was almost sure he detected a glimmer of interest for himself in Joy's dark eyes—a soft feminine response to his unspoken, quiet yearning for happiness, love, and a normal life.

Had he been completely mistaken?

Wearily, he leaned his elbows on the saber-scarred table. The memory of the Indians of the Outer Place dangled in his mind—the filth of their quarters, the emaciated bodies, the vacant stares in watery, bloodshot eyes. Was that to be his destiny? Was that where the lure of whiskey would lead him?

Red Shirt spoke it.

And in his heart, James knew it was true.

For the first time since returning from the War, he wondered if he could live without whiskey. And for the first time since returning from the War, he wanted to live without it.

Red Shirt said James needn't tackle such a big job alone; God would help him, if and when he asked.

⌇

A loud, insistent rapping roused James from his slumber at the dining room table, where he nodded off. Someone at the front door? With Jeb and his wife, Missy, in town on errands, there was no one to answer the knock. James quickly thrust his hand through his hair and went to greet his visitor—a rare occurrence these days.

"Judge Wilcox! What brings you to Plumtree?"

The short, balding man was a friend of the Sheffield family since before James was born. He took off his hat and stepped into the foyer. "Good day, James. I've come to try to talk some sense into you."

James felt like a chastened schoolboy as he led the judge into what had once been a richly furnished parlor. He flushed with silent humiliation and offered the judge one of the two remaining chairs.

"I'll get straight to the point," said Orlando Wilcox as he perched on the edge of a blue wingback. "Jeb told me about your gambling debt to Porter Hopkins."

James stared at the floor, ashamed to meet the judge's probing gaze.

"I've known the Sheffields since your daddy first moved to these parts, son, so I feel as if you're family."

James nervously tapped his boot on the only Oriental rug left at Plumtree.

"Jeb says as part of the gambling debt, you promised your niece's hand in marriage to that vile…reprobate…and that to save herself from becoming Porter's bride, she ran away." Wilcox sighed and shook his head. "What were you thinking, son?"

James shrugged and resigned himself to the lecture. Whatever Wilcox was about to say, he had it coming—and then some.

"I want you to know that those so-called contracts are illegal," the judge went on, his voice firm. "Hopkins has no claim on this plantation. As for young Drewry—" his voice dropped to a near whisper, "—we can only pray that the Lord will protect her until she has a mind to contact you again."

James continued to stare at the rug beneath his feet. A lump formed in his throat. What if Drewry never contacted him again? What if she came to harm because of his greed?

The judge reached out and rested a hand on James's shoulder. Squeezing slightly, he said, "You are in bondage to alcohol, James, just as your father, Abraham, before you. And like your father, drink is causing you to commit despicable and immoral deeds. It's hurting everyone who loves you."

James swallowed hard. In the past, he would have leapt to his feet, prickling with defensiveness, and ordered the old judge from his home. Instead, he sat in silence, strangely moved that the man took the time to ride all the way out to Plumtree to confront him.

"I don't mind admitting that it breaks my heart to see what you've become," Wilcox continued. Glancing around the room, he added in a quiet voice, "And what's become of this fine old home."

"Where is the bright-eyed, good-natured lad I remember? Have you completely given up, James? Have you handed over your soul to the demon alcohol?"

Finally, James was able to meet the old man's concerned gaze. Where was the James Sheffield of days gone by? What happened to his happy-go-lucky personality? His kindheartedness? His nose-to-the-grindstone work ethic? James had no answers for the judge's questions...or his own. He shook his head slowly. "I don't know," he said. "I just plain don't know."

Suddenly, the judge was on his feet, his boots thumping across the threadbare carpeting. "I'll tell you where James Sheffield is!" he thundered. "At the bottom of a bottle, that's where!" He whirled around and stomped over to where James sat, head in hands, pausing in front of the faded blue chair. "Drink ruined your father, and now it's ruining you. Don't cave into it, James." Wilcox punched the air with a chubby fist. "Show some gumption! Stand up and fight!"

James studied the earnest, leathery face. The eyes, clear and honest as a cloudless summer sky, glittered with frustration at James's plight. But there was fatherly concern there, too. And pain.

The judge raised a silvery brow and narrowed his eyes. "You can do it, son."

James exhaled loudly and shook his head. "I have tried. And I failed.... Now I wouldn't know where to begin."

"I'll tell you where!" the judge bellowed. "Right here, right now! You'll give it up, is what! Total abstinence, that's the key!"

Abstinence? No whiskey at all? Ever again? The thought sent his heart to pounding. He licked his lips. "Surely I can cut down...."

But Wilcox waved off his lame suggestion. "Total abstinence, James. It's the only way."

James was on his feet now, too, pacing the area in front of the marble fireplace. Suddenly, his thirst for whiskey seemed huge and unquenchable. "But I have a strong will," he protested. "I can cut back. I know I can...."

Wilcox blocked his path and put his hands on James's shoulders. Looking him squarely in the eye, the older man said, "No. You can't. It's bad enough you think you can get away with lying to me, James. But you're lying to yourself. That's the worst lie of all."

James blinked in silent response.

"You can do it. I know you can. But you can't do it alone."

You can't do it alone.... You can't do it alone.... The words echoed in James's brain. Hadn't Red Shirt said the same thing?

"God will help you," finished the judge. "Pray, James. Pray as you've never prayed before. This is no schoolboy crush, nor a Spelling Bee. This is your life we're talking about, son. Can't you see that you're killing yourself, an ounce of whiskey at a time?"

The judge gave James a good shaking. "Wake up, boy! Do what's right...before it's too late. Think about it, son. Now I'll see myself out."

When the old man left, James dropped into the chair, taking in what Wilcox said. To live the rest of his life without ever taking another drink? No more whiskey...forever? He couldn't imagine how he would resist temptation that long.

He didn't know how long he sat there, musing over his past. At last he rose and wandered the empty mansion, once filled with cherished possessions and brimming with life and warmth.

What Wilcox said was true, after all. James was killing himself, one golden ounce at a time. Worse, he was killing the love others once felt for him.

He thought of Joy, bound forever to the cold, detached minister. Of Jeb and Missy, who stood by him despite his cruel treatment. Of Drewry...his only living relative—the niece he drove away with his selfish scheming.

Could it ever be the same? Could he ever have again the joys of the old life?

Of everything the old judge said, one phrase resounded loudest in James's mind: "I know you have feelings for Joy McGuire, James. And anyone with eyes can see that Matthew Frost has set his cap for her." Wilcox covered his bald head with his derby. "But if you let her get away, you're more lost than I thought!"

FIVE

With the men away on a hunting expedition, the Suscataway village hummed with the quiet precision of a well-tuned instrument. Beyond the palisade, in fields slashed from the forest, lay gently rolling patches of corn and wheat, beans and squash. The plants were lovingly tended by the women and children, whose hand-hewn tools of bone and wood kept the weeds at bay and protected the roots of each delicate plant from the harsh, baking sun.

Joy's Indian mother taught her how to make those crude tools. She remembered well how to use dampened strips of leather to secure a handle to the business end of a shovel, so that when the leather dried, it shortened, forming a bond so tight it would last through several uses before requiring an adjustment. Joy learned to make leather garments, too, fashioned from well-scraped deer hides, pounded soft with hammer and stone, until it draped like cloth in supple folds. Colorful beads and shells, sewn to the hems and necklines of shirts and pants and dresses, stamped each garment with the personality of its wearer.

The men had been gone nearly three days now. When they returned, they would bring with them deer, rabbit, squirrel, and wild turkey. It had been a good year, thus far. Plenty of rain, following a mild winter, meant that the birds and animals found along the banks of the Gunpowder had grown plump on a steady diet of berries, nuts, and vegetation. In preparation for the return of the hunters, the women and children built cooking fires in the center of the village and cleaned out the long houses where skins and meats would be hung to dry.

As Joy moved through the village, pride swelled her heart, for these resourceful people were her people. They learned to make do with very little, to survive harsh winters and blazing summers. They learned to live in peace alongside the White Man—who, one day, sought their help in adapting to life in this new world; and the next, it seemed, sought to force them from their homeland.

Gray Hawk signed a treaty with an official-looking representative of President Lincoln. The contract assured the government that there would be no uprising from the gentle Suscataways. It gave the Indians no such assurance. It was only because Gray Hawk agreed to keep his people within the boundaries drawn by the new rulers of his former homeland that they were allowed to continue living in harmony on the outskirts of a well-established American settlement.

Joy greatly respected and admired Chief Gray Hawk. She was glad he hadn't accompanied the men on this hunt, for she had much to discuss with him on this bleak day. "Do you have a moment to advise me?" she asked when at last she spotted her old friend.

His white teeth flashed in his tanned face when he smiled at her. "For you, Laughing Eyes, I always have time."

She loved the Indian name he gave her on the day she and her father returned to Freetown. "You wear a smile from your soul to your eyes," he had told her. "We will call you Laughing Eyes."

Now, sitting with Gray Hawk in his hut, she inhaled the crisp aroma of his tobacco. He sat on a crude wooden bench, his mocassined feet crossed at the ankles, as he puffed a long-stemmed, feathered pipe. He motioned for her to sit on the stool across from him. "I can see that you are troubled," he said. "What has dimmed the light in your laughing eyes?"

She took a deep breath. How well he knew her! "James Sheffield."

Gray Hawk nodded. "Ah, yes. The man who dances to the music of the whiskey." His dark gaze bored into hers. "Do you love this man?"

Joy gasped. "Why, no! Of course not! It's...it's just.... Well, he seems to need guidance—both spiritual and earthly—and he seems to think he can find both in me." She folded her hands in her lap. "I fear I'm not strong enough or wise enough to give him what he needs."

Again Gray Hawk nodded. "You helped my son, and many others besides. Red Shirt would still live in the Outer Place if not for you. It was your constant patience and prayers that saved my son. What makes you think you cannot save this Sheffield man?"

Joy shook her head. "He's different from most. Stronger. More stubborn. And he's been under the influence longer than Red Shirt was when I met him."

"What has that to do with anything? Running Deer and I had given Red Shirt up as lost, and he was cursed with the craving for whiskey only a short time before you came to us."

What Gray Hawk said made sense. It was not the passage of time, but the depth of dependency that made the difference.

"You must accept your limitations, Laughing Eyes. God has blessed you with a great gift in making you an instrument of His peace. But you can only bring God's healing to those who wish to be healed."

Joy thought about that for a moment. "But what if James is too far gone to realize he needs healing?"

He leaned forward and placed a weathered hand on her forearm. "This will be hard for you to hear, Laughing Eyes, and I do not wish to hurt you. But in the end, no matter what anyone said or did, it was alcohol your mother called 'lord.' He hesitated, and gave her arm an affectionate little squeeze. "Have you considered that James may be like your mother?"

Joy sighed deeply. Yes, she thought of that...more often than she cared to admit. And it pained her to think it, for she liked James and genuinely wanted to help him. But what if, in trying to save him, she lost herself?

As if he could read her thoughts, Gray Hawk spoke up. "You must be alert, for if you are not, you will be pulled into the mire with him. He must choose life over death. You cannot make him choose; it is something he must do for himself alone."

Again her friend spoke the truth. Joy stood, leaned over and placed a gentle kiss on his cheek. "You have been like a father to me—those times when my own father is far away, doing church business," she said. "I cherish our talks, and I'll give your advice much thoughtful prayer."

"And you are like a daughter to me. Go now, and begin the hard work of saving your James Sheffield."

⌒

Your James Sheffield, Gray Hawk said. Joy smiled in spite of herself. But the smile quickly faded. Under other circumstances, she would have been proud to claim James as her man. Under these conditions, however....

Oh, how she missed her father! If only Samuel were not in Philadelphia again...Joy knew she should be accustomed to his absences by now. Still, she yearned to hear his suggestions as to what she should do about her dilemma.

She snuggled deeper in her overstuffed chair and stroked the calico cat in her lap. The cat wandered into her yard a few days ago and decided to adopt Joy. Winding herself about Joy's ankles, she looked up with round golden eyes and a contented purr...and won Joy's heart. Soon afterward, she dubbed the calico "Iffen," for in the words of a homespun homily, she told her: "You comes when I call...iffen you feels like it."

Glad for the company and for the creature's genuine warmth, Joy smiled. Iffen purred contently as she scratched her velvety ears. "What am I going to do?" she asked the cat.

She answered with a wide-eyed meow, then squinted up at her and rubbed her head against her open palm.

Sighing, Joy leaned her head back against the chair's pillowy headrest and closed her eyes. Gray Hawk's words rang loud in her head: *In the end, it was Whiskey your mother called "lord."*

Memories drifted in and out of her mind, memories of good days long gone. How ironic, Joy mused, that Ruth turned to whiskey on the advice of the knowledgeable and respected Dr. Louis Ludwig. Her mother was at a neighbor's house, helping the doctor deliver a baby. On the way home, she tripped on a gnarled tree root. It was no simple break, Dr. Ludwig told them. "Compound fracture," he called it. Since she'd be in considerable pain for weeks, he prescribed a sip of whiskey now and again to help dull the throbbing.

It was amazing how quickly Ruth and Whiskey became friends. Long before her leg healed, she fell countless other times, having taken one too many "sips" to ease the pain. By the time she healed physically, her mind was far more handicapped than her leg had ever been.

For years, Joy watched her mother's steady decline. For years, she watched her father struggle with his own pain.

She watched as whiskey smothered the love that bound her parents together. And she watched, helplessly, as it dealt the final deadly blow that ended her mother's life.

Ruth's drowning so affected Samuel that, when his superiors announced a need for a pastoral overseer, he volunteered for the position. In those first years after Ruth's death, Samuel and Joy became like vagabonds, nomads who drifted from place to place. Just when Joy began to feel comfortable somewhere, it was time to move on. It wasn't until they came to Freetown and she started working with the Suscataways that her father agreed to settle down. This move back to their original home, she hoped, would be their last. She loved the sleepy little town, its pristine streets and tidy buildings, its friendly residents....

And now...handsome, haunted James Sheffield.

Iffen stretched languidly on her lap, then leapt onto the floor and pranced toward the door. Meowing pitifully, she begged for her freedom.

Joy leaned over to pat her head before letting her out. *If only James could be free of whiskey this easily*, she thought as Iffen bounded across the yard.

◜◞

Joy tidied her skirt and re-braided her hair, then headed for her father's office to return the book she borrowed that morning.

She found Matthew, deep in thought, gazing through the open window, booted feet resting on the windowsill. "Are you still here?" she asked when she came through the door.

His feet hit the floor with a thud. "Land sakes, Joy, you've shaved ten years off the last half of my life!" he croaked, gathering his composure. "You move like a cat."

Joy giggled at the thought of this tall, muscular man, scared out of his wits by a woman half his size. "I'm here to return Father's book. What about you?"

Matthew stood and adjusted the black, slipknot tie at his throat. "I'm writing Sunday's sermon."

Joy's brow furrowed. "You mean the words don't come to you in a moment of Divine Inspiration?" she teased. "You actually have to work for them?"

Matthew frowned.

"I know, I know," she said. "Shouldn't make light of a heavy subject." If Matthew said it once, she'd heard it a thousand times. "Relax, Matthew Frost! You'll live longer, and you might make a few more friends besides."

He glared at her. "I have no time for friends and fun. I've the Lord's work to do." He paused, eyeing her meaningfully. "I'm thinking you could do with a little less frivolity yourself, Joy McGuire."

She rolled her eyes. "Show me in the Good Book where it says it's a sin to laugh, and I'll gladly wear a sour face like yours."

"Make sport of me if you like. I can take it. In fact, I delight in it! *I will show him how great things he must suffer for my name's sake,*" he quoted the apostle Paul.

"Oh, Matthew!" Joy said, waving off his pious protest. "When have you ever suffered in His name?" Matthew turned his back on her. "You are a coldhearted woman, Joy McGuire. Makes me wonder if we're a proper match, after all."

Her jaw dropped and her eyes widened. "'A proper match!' You and me? Are you speaking of…marriage?"

Slowly, he turned around to face her. "I've discussed the matter several times with your father," he said, narrowing his slanted green eyes. "He seems to agree we're right for each other."

Indignation bubbled deep within at the thought of the two of them planning her future, without even bothering to invite her to the meeting! "How dare you make such plans without consulting me. I'm a grown woman, and I can choose my own life mate, thank you."

Matthew threw back his blond head and laughed. "Of course you can," he said, his tone edged with sarcasm. "A mate like James Sheffield, I suppose."

Truthfully, the thought crossed her mind a time or two, after witnessing James's rescue of Little Crow, for example, or observing his tender way with the Suscataway children, or seeing him work side by side with the men of the village. For all his bluff and bluster, James had a sweet, sensitive side....

"Your silence betrays you, Joy."

"On the contrary!" she shot back. "My silence only proves that I know better than to argue with a know-it-all." With that, she turned on her heel and stormed off.

Matthew trailed in her wake. "You can't seriously be entertaining thoughts of a future with that gutter tramp, can you?"

"I can't believe you followed me into the street. Leave me alone, Matthew Frost, before I lose my temper and say something we'll both regret."

"Just as soon as you convince me you're not romantically interested in that...man."

"How can you call yourself a minister of God's Word when you deliberately turn your back on one who needs the message so desperately?"

"Don't make me laugh. That whiskey-swilling bum would fall asleep if I spoke to him of God and angels."

Her chin quivered with pent-up fury and frustration. *"Judge not according to appearance, but judge righteous judgment."*

"Don't quote Scripture to me! Not in defense of that heathen!"

"He's not a heathen! He believes in God, the same as you and I."

"Not as I do," Matthew countered. "If he believed as I believe, he'd have no battle with the bottle."

Joy waited a moment before speaking. "At least," she said, her voice dangerously low, "when James celebrates his victory, he'll have something to take pride in. There's no glory in your self-righteous indignation, Matthew Frost. No honor in a prideful spirit."

On that note, she marched away, leaving him standing in the middle of the street.

"I'll pray for you!" he shouted after her. "You're going to need it if you continue to befriend that man!"

As angry as the arrogant young preacher made her, Joy knew that Matthew was at least partly right. She did need prayer...if she expected to meet with any success at all concerning James Sheffield.

SIX

"Father...I didn't expect you back until tomorrow!" Smiling in greeting, Joy sprang up from her solitary dinner.

"Ah, girl, ye're a sight fer sore eyes." The Reverend Samuel McGuire crossed the humble kitchen with a lightness of foot that belied his heft and his fifty-five years.

The native of Ireland's County Mayo spent most of his adult life in servitude to the Lord; most of the past six years overseeing the young ministers who brought the gospel to the people of his adopted land.

Joy hugged her broad-shouldered father, brushing her cheek against his fluffy gray beard as she did so often as a child. With some effort, she repressed her anger that, without her knowledge, he discussed her marital future with Matthew Frost. "Sit down and I'll get you a bowl of stew and some hot cornbread."

"Just what a man needs after a long journey." Samuel dropped his book-laden satchel near the door. "A hearty meal and warm conversation." He dropped onto the seat of a rough-hewn wooden chair. "'Tis good to be home, daughter."

And it was good to have him home, Joy admitted as she ladled the steaming beefy broth into an earthenware bowl, then placed it on the table, flanked by a white linen napkin and a big silver spoon. She poured him a mug of hot tea before sitting across from him. "Save room for some apple pie later," she warned him with a wink.

Samuel patted his ample belly. "Another good reason to give thanks," he said, chuckling as he bowed his head and offered a simple grace.

Her father's directness was one of the things she loved most about him, Joy mused, deciding to approach him now. "I need your advice about a very important matter, but I don't rightly know where to begin...."

When his patient smile encouraged her to continue, Joy found the words suddenly flowing. She recounted the rumors about James's drinking, his bravery the day Little Crow nearly drowned, the disappointment she felt the night he sent her sprawling into the mud....

Samuel's gray eyes narrowed thoughtfully as he buttered a chunk of cornbread. "Sounds like a man with the weight of the world on 'is shoulders. Have you taken 'im to the Outer Place?"

"Yes, and Red Shirt spoke with him at length."

He nodded his approval. "Good. The fella needs to get an eyeful of what'll become of 'im if he don't soon change 'is ways."

Joy took a sip of her tea. "It concerns me a bit that Little Crow follows him everywhere. Why, he almost idolizes James Sheffield."

Samuel laughed softly. "No need to worry on that score, daughter. The boy's admiration can be a good thing. When a lad looks to a man for guidance, it forces the man to behave more like a man." Grinning mischievously, he leaned closer. "Now, and what are your feelings for this James Sheffield?"

She felt the color rise in her cheeks. Why would her father ask such a question, Joy wondered, when he already discussed— on several occasions, according to Matthew—her future with the assistant pastor? "Though I plainly see Mr. Sheffield's faults," she said carefully, "I find that I have...I'm afraid I have developed, uh... an attachment...for him."

Samuel put down his spoon and fixed a somber gaze on her. "I needn't remind you of the hell your mother put us through, daughter, because of strong drink."

The pain in his eyes made her look quickly away. Yes, she remembered all too well how they suffered, watching Ruth die a slow death.

He leaned an elbow on the table and wagged a thick forefinger under her nose. "Ye say you're afraid ye have feelings for the man? Well, 'tis good you're afraid, because unless James Sheffield reforms, he can bring ye nothing but misery."

Joy stared into her bowl and stirred aimlessly.

Samuel reached across the table and covered her tiny hand with his brawny one. "You can point the way, sweet Joy of me heart, and you can provide encouragement and prayer, but in the end, 'tis his decision to make."

Joy relished the comfort of her father's words and lifted her eyes to meet his. "I'll pray for James," she said softly. Then, shrugging, she added miserably, "What more can I do?"

Samuel patted her hand, then took another bite of his stew, chewing thoughtfully. "Perhaps I'm overstepping even a father's prerogative here," he said after awhile, "but have ye considered Matthew Frost as a beau? He's a respectable Christian man...."

Joy tensed. Would he tell her now that he and Matthew plotted her future, as if she were some addlepated young girl who couldn't choose a proper mate for herself? "Oh, Father," she said, frustration forcing her voice an octave higher than usual, "Matthew may be a man and he may be a Christian, but he's as cold as his name! Why would I want to wed him?"

Samuel threw back his head and laughed heartily. "And who said anything about a wedding, now?"

Joy's brow furrowed in confusion. "But—but I thought you and Matthew decided…"

Midway between his bowl and his lips, Samuel's spoon halted as he anticipated what she was about to say. "Matthew and I have decided nothing, daughter. Where did you get such a ridiculous notion?"

"From Matthew, of course. He told me just yesterday that the two of you discussed it at length. From what he said, you wanted us to set a date."

"All I want, dear daughter," Samuel began, choosing his words carefully, "is yer happiness. There's no denyin' I think Matthew would make you happier than James Sheffield—at least in his present condition…"

He paused, then added, "Continue to pray for the lad. I'll pray, too. But give 'im the freedom to embrace sobriety or reject it. Let 'im exercise his own free will, as God intended."

$\backsim$

From time to time, she saw him at the Suscataway village, visiting with Red Shirt or Little Crow. From a distance, Joy studied the interchange between her friends and James. It gave her great satisfaction to watch his face, alight with pleasure as he played with the children, or grim with determination as he learned how to skin a rabbit for the stew pot. Not once had she seen any sign that he was drinking the night before—no swollen bloodshot eyes, no puffy face, and—when he was near her—no odor of alcohol on his breath.

One morning, Joy could not resist asking James why he spent so much time at the Suscataway village. Surely with his resolve to turn Plumtree Orchards around, he had plenty to do at home.

He merely smiled in that way that made her weak in the knees and said, "Yes, but I need to remind myself—daily it seems of what

I might become if I don't get hold of this problem I have with whiskey. Seeing the braves in the Outer Place..."

He told her in great detail about his meeting with Judge Wilcox, and she found herself impressed with James's openness. Though she hated seeing the tortured expression on his handsome face, it gladdened her heart to hear him confess his problem.

"When was the last time you had a drink, James?" she asked.

He flushed and stared at some distant spot beyond her shoulder. "This morning," he admitted, startling her with his honesty once again. He met her gaze, unflinching. "But only a few swallows."

It was a good sign, she knew. If he hadn't already planted both feet firmly on the road to recovery, he'd have denied this most recent bout with the enemy. The fact that he was willing to talk about it was most definitely a good sign.

She studied his face, the handsome features showing signs of his struggle. Whenever something was troubling her, she recalled, she found solace on a bluff overlooking the Gunpowder. From her rocky perch high above the town, she felt nearer the Creator, somehow, as if by merely reaching up, she might be able to touch Him. Moved by James's efforts to overcome his bondage to drink, Joy decided to share the peace and tranquility of this private place with him.

Impulsively, she grabbed his hand and tugged him down a narrow woodland path.

"Whoa!" he protested. "Where are you taking me?" "To my secret hideaway," she called over her shoulder. "You can see the world from there."

James allowed himself to be led along for what seemed endless moments. The only sounds, save for their hushed footfalls on the leaf-covered, loamy earth, were occasional birdcalls and the singing of crickets and locusts. Here the underbrush grew lush and luxuriant, and the scent of wild blackberries tickled his nostrils.

For some time, the thick growth of pines overhead darkened the brightness of the day. Then, suddenly, almost without warning, the sun burst through as they stepped into a clearing.

"Well," Joy said, encompassing their surroundings with a grand sweep of her hand, "what do you think?"

Stunned by the sight of her, silhouetted against the cloudless blue sky, James could see nothing else. Her long, sable hair fell away from her face, draping her shoulders like a shimmering black cape. *You're lovely,* he mused. *The most beautiful thing I've ever seen....*

"James," she interrupted, stamping a foot to claim his attention, "you aren't looking in the right place! Tell me what you think of my secret place?"

James forced his gaze to the surrounding area. Towering pines formed the backdrop of the vista ahead. Underfoot, springy green moss cushioned the stony ground. The hushed rushing of the Gunpowder, slipping over fallen logs and around huge rocks, whispered far below.

"It's...very nice," he said after a time.

"Nice!" she echoed, planting her fists on her hips. "Is that all you have to say for it?"

James couldn't help but smile. That this diminutive person could contain so much sheer delight in living, that her joy spilled over to touch everyone she met, filled him with wonder. *Joy.* Her parents named her well.

"I doubt that I have ever seen a more beautiful sight," he said truthfully, taking care to cast his gaze in the direction of the view stretching out before them. But for the life of him, he didn't know how she could expect him to appreciate the beauty of the landscape when she was standing there—her radiance blinding him to the rest.

She seemed satisfied with his response, however, and turned to look out upon the world around them. "You can see all the way to Pennsylvania from here," she began, pointing, "and on a really clear day, you can face this way and see West Virginia!"

It took very little effort to comply with her unspoken directive. It was a fantastic scene, indeed.

"I used to come up here as a child," she said softly, her hands clasped behind her back.

"But I thought you were new to Freetown...."

She lowered her head, and when she did, her hair fell forward, veiling her face. James resisted the urge to reach out and tuck one silken strand behind her ear.

"I was born here," she explained, settling herself on a boulder, "in the same house where I'm living now." She turned to face him. "My mother, Ruth, was a Suscataway. My father was a young missionary when they met." She grinned, crinkling her nose and sending his heart soaring. "It was love at first sight, I suppose. There were two wedding ceremonies—one in the village and one in town."

For a long time, Joy said nothing more. James, unwilling to disturb her thoughts, sat quietly beside her on the big rock and waited for her to continue.

Finally, Joy sighed deeply. "I was twelve years old when we left Freetown, less than a month after we buried Mama. For six years, Father and I traveled up and down the East Coast, visiting churches in small towns and cities, but never calling any of them home.

"And then one day, as if he could read my heart, Father decided it was time to come back." She shrugged and smoothed her skirts.

"So now you hold down the fort, and your father travels alone," James observed.

Joy nodded. She leaned forward to pluck a rosebud from a tangled mass of wild roses growing over an outcropping of rock. She closed her eyes to inhale the delicate scent, and James's heart beat erratically as her lashes dusted her cheek.

In the next instant, she recoiled, bringing one finger to her mouth. "Ouch! I've gouged myself with a thorn."

James held her hand in his and inspected the wound. "I think the patient will live," he assured, gently dabbing at the drop of blood with a clean white handkerchief.

"Guess that's what I get for trying to rob Mother Nature." Joy giggled and popped the injured forefinger back into her mouth.

James reached behind her and plucked another flower, its petals precisely the same rich red as the droplet of blood. "Roses are by far one of God's loveliest creations." He dropped the flower in her lap and added, "But He did some of His finest work when He created you."

Joy searched the crystalline blue depths of his eyes for the truth about James Sheffield. She heard in town that, before the War, he was a fun-loving, honorable man, devoted to family, business, and church. She found it hard to believe a man could be loyal one day, lecherous the next. What horrible things had he witnessed on the battlefield, what awful deeds had he been forced to do? The ghosts that haunted James Sheffield must be more than terrifying—they must be powerful, indeed, to have held him prisoner for so long.

Joy touched the velvety rose to her cheek. *He has a good heart. Maybe he's known only the thorns rather than the soft and beautiful things of life,* she reasoned.

Without further thought, Joy broke the thorns from the stem, then took James's hand and wrapped his fingers around it. "Here, it's safe now. You needn't fear the thorns any longer, James."

James blanched. Did she think him that weak-spirited? So far gone that he needed a woman to protect him from life's hurts?

He scanned the angles and planes of her smooth face. There was no deception in it—only the offer of friendship and devotion.

For some unaccountable reason, he knew that this woman would stand by him, no matter what the Matthew Frosts of this world thought of him. He wanted to throw his arms around her and crush her to him, to proclaim his undying love.

What stopped him was a sobering thought: She deserved far better than James Sheffield! Even Matthew Frost, with his cold-eyed arrogance, was better for her than he. *At least*, James told himself, *Frost has no demons to battle....*

"Have you made the promise yet, James?" Her soft question was barely more audible than the gentle breeze that rustled the pine needles.

He fumbled with the rose, confusion rumpling his brow. "What promise?"

"Have you vowed to give up whiskey, once and for all?"

James's cheeks reddened yet again as he shook his head. "Not in the way you mean, I suppose. But I've promised to try...."

She slanted him a look that made his knees go weak. She believed him. Overjoyed, James could only nod and swallow the lump that formed in his throat.

"I brought you here," she said, sandwiching his big hand between her tiny ones, "because I found peace in this place when I was a child. There are still days when I need to come here." She paused, looking out over the vast expanse of land, then added shyly, "I've never shared this spot with anyone before. Not even my father...."

He let the meaning of that declaration sink in, hardly daring to believe what he hoped she was saying. But she was not finished.

"Do you feel it, too, James? The closeness to God? It's almost as if you could reach right out and touch His face...." Her breathy voice trailed off in a reverent whisper.

In all honesty, he did feel a certain contentment here in her secret place. But James was pretty sure it was not the awesome beauty of God's creation alone that gave him this contented feeling. No, he rather suspected it had something to do with being this near a certain earthly angel.

Joy leaned forward, pressing him for an answer. Heart racing, he struggled to phrase the truth in such a way that it would be acceptable to this woman he so longed to please. "Ye—es. I suppose I do feel closer to God here."

His answer did please her—that much was evident from the smile that broke on her face. "Good," she said matter-of-factly, "because the next time you're tempted to listen to the bottle, I want you to come here and listen to God instead."

Abruptly Joy stood and headed for the path. As she ducked under a low-lying pine branch, she stopped, turned, and frowned back at him. "Well, are you going to sit there all morning, or are you going into town with me?"

With that, she disappeared into the woods, leaving James—stunned and slack-jawed—still sitting alone on a boulder in her secret place.

SEVEN

James couldn't remember working harder, or feeling more satisfied at the end of the day. At least, not since long before the War. More and more often, he found himself visiting the Suscataway village, helping Joy teach the children, or simply standing on the sidelines, watching her perform her little miracles with them.

A particularly bright spot in the days he spent at her side was Little Crow, who dogged his heels. It was the first time James experienced such idolatry. But ever since the day he rescued the boy, the dark-haired child had been his shadow. Being the object of a growing boy's admiration gave James much to ponder. And more than once, it had given him the incentive he needed to stay on the straight and narrow. Never knowing when Little Crow might pop up, it occurred to James that his obsession with drink could well be the ruination of that innocent child.

But more than anything or anyone else, James thought of Joy and her zeal to improve the lives of her people. She did these good deeds with quiet acceptance, without attempting to change the Suscataways, as so many of the townsfolk had. "Good deeds," she explained when he called her on it, "are most effective when performed in secrecy."

He thought about this for a long time after returning to Plumtree Orchards. There, in the sparsely furnished parlor, James began to understand that God smiled upon those who gave freely of their time and talents, with no thought for what they'd take with them when the good deed was done. There'd be no praise, no accolades, no glorified speeches of gratitude, no medals of honor....

No medals of honor, James thought with a self-deprecating smile. *Not that I have anything to fear on that score....* Disgusted, he glared at his left boot, encasing what was left of his mangled foot. He grimaced, not so much with the physical discomfort, but in recognition of the reason he would be forever maimed. No, there would be no medals of honor for James Sheffield.

A soft knock interrupted his reverie, and James limped across the wide marble foyer to throw open one massive oak door. The tarnished brass hinges squealed in the empty, echoing space.

"Little Crow! What on earth are you doing here? Why, it's nearly twenty miles to the village. How'd you get here?"

"I walked, of course," the boy announced, stepping boldly into the house.

"But it'll be dark soon. Your mother and father will be worried about you."

"They knew I would be safe here with you." James's brow furrowed. "And they didn't try to stop you?"

Little Crow frowned in puzzlement. "Why should they stop me?"

Because I'm the town drunk. Because I might lead you astray. Because I'm a terrible example, and you shouldn't be alone with me.... He kept his thoughts to himself, however, and changed the subject. "Have you had any supper?"

"No." The boy's grin clearly said that if invited, he'd gladly join James for a meal.

Arms akimbo, James surveyed the mischievous child. "Well, let's see what Missy can rustle up." He led the way down the hall to the kitchen.

Inside, he sidled up to the cook stove and peeked into a large iron pot. "Ah, chicken stew and dumplings, it appears...."

The boy licked his lips. "Dumplin's are my fav'rite!" Then, "Who's Missy?"

"Don't tell me you've never met Jeb's pretty wife?"

A lanky, dark-skinned woman poked her head in from the keeping room. "Who be sayin' my name?"

James waved her into the kitchen. "Come meet my good friend, Little Crow."

"H'lo," the boy said.

"H'lo, yourself." Missy folded her arms across her bony chest and faked an angry scowl. "What you doin' so far from home at this time of day? You is sure to get lost goin' home."

"Oh, no, I won't," Little Crow insisted. "I know those woods like the back of my hand."

"Soon as this boy gets a good hot meal in his belly, I'll take him home," James said.

Missy turned her back to them and busied herself by filling two pottery bowls with the steaming stew. "Seem like the blind lead in' the blind, if you ask me," she muttered under her breath.

James ignored the remark, knowing that Missy had every right to doubt his ability to maneuver the woods after dark. Well, he had no intention of going back by way of the forest anyway. Instead, he'd hitch up the old coach—if its axles weren't too rusted to make the trip—and deliver the child in fine style.

"Set yo'sefs down an' eat," Missy instructed sternly, "before it gets cold." With that, she headed back to the keeping room. "Got to tend my kettle of apple butter."

After sopping up the last of his stew with a fluffy biscuit, the boy announced, "I'm gonna go to college up North and learn how to be a doctor when I grow up, so I can come back and take care of everybody in the village. Joy says if we live upright lives, and work hard, and pray, God will reward us with good things."

James tensed involuntarily. *Live right, work hard, and pray. So that's her view on the world, is it?* James asked himself. *No wonder she believes there's good in you, man! She's blinded by child-like innocence!*

"We'd better get you home, boy," James said, abruptly changing the subject. "Let's see about hitching the horses to the wagon."

When they were less than half a mile from the village road, Little Crow began chattering happily about his future plans. He intended to grow up big and strong, he said, just like James. He'd go off to war and fight for freedom, just like James. He'd learn to fight and curse and sing loud, bawdy ballads, and find himself two floozies, one for each arm…just like James.

James's face burned with humiliation. If a child could peg him so accurately, what must a woman like Joy be thinking? Was her kindness merely her gentle way of dealing with hopeless drunkards? Had she meant anything she said in the "secret place," or had her pretty words been spoken solely for the benefit of his poor, wounded soul?

He'd worry about that later. Right now, he had to set this boy straight, once and for all. James tugged at the reins and brought the wagon to a grinding halt in the middle of the dusty road. Bracing his big hands on Little Crow's narrow shoulders, he said sternly, "Now you listen to me, and you listen good. If you grow up and become a man like me, you'll never see your dreams come true." He gave the boy's shoulders a little shake. "You've heard what they say about me in town. Folks think I'm vile and evil. Ladies cross to the other side of the street to avoid being on the same boardwalk with me. And they're right to do it!"

Little Crow's eyes filled with tears. "But Mr. James…you saved my life."

James released the child, giving him a little shove. Then with a loud, angry laugh, he said with a sneer, "That! Why, that was an accident! You don't think for a minute I planned to be a hero, do you? You're just lucky I was on my way into town when I heard you calling for help. If I was on my way home, I'd have been too drunk to see the river, let alone jump into it to save your sorry hide."

Little Crow's tears flowed freely now. "I don't care what you say!" he shouted. "You *did* save my life! You did! My father says you're a hero, and my father never lies!" With that, he leapt from the wagon and ran as fast as his little legs would carry him. In seconds, he was out of sight.

It broke James's heart to have shattered some of the boy's innocence in those moments. But James would sleep more soundly that night, knowing Little Crow wouldn't attempt to emulate the town drunk any longer! And maybe, if he applied a bit of Joy's advice to his own sorry life, he'd develop the strength of character it would take to change.

Tomorrow, he vowed, *will be my first full day without whiskey. But for now*, he told himself, rummaging under the buckboard for one of the two full bottles he stowed there once he harnessed the horses, *it's business as usual.*

James uncorked the first bottle and took a long swallow, then clucked the horses into action and turned the wagon around. He didn't want to think about what he'd been forced to admit to Little Crow. Didn't want to deal with the truth for a moment longer. With any luck, he'd be dead drunk before he got home.

～

James woke for the first time in years without the familiar throb of a headache pounding behind his eyes. He sat up and stretched, then yawned loudly.

Realizing that his mouth was dry, his first thought was to quench that thirst with a stiff drink. Then he remembered why he hadn't gotten stinking drunk last night, as usual. Falling asleep halfway between the village road and Plumtree was the only thing that prevented him from emptying both bottles of whiskey. As it was, he only downed a quarter of the first one when Jeb found him at the end of the long, winding drive.

"Them hosses was grazin' in the sweet grass when I foun' you," Jeb had said, gently shaking his friend awake. "Get on up to bed, Mistah James, while I take these hardworkin' animals to the stable."

For the life of him, James couldn't figure out why he did as Jeb suggested and gone straight to bed, leaving both bottles of whiskey in the wagon. Shrugging aside the mystery, James rubbed his bearded chin, then climbed from the bed. As always, he refused to look at his gnarled left foot, but covered the hideous thing in a thick white sock, then stuffed it into his boot.

At the dresser, he poured water from the crockery pitcher into a matching bowl, dipped both hands into the refreshing liquid, then splashed his face and neck. Leaning closer to the mirror, James inspected his grizzled reflection.

It was time for a fresh start, he decided, rifling in the drawer beneath the water basin. *How long had it been since he used the silver-handled razor?* he wondered, unsheathing it from its brown leather case. He held it aloft, seeing the glint of the morning sun on its finely honed, single-edged blade.

In the same drawer, where he stored the razor, was his old shaving mug. Quickly, before he could change his mind, he mixed shaving cream, whipping it into a lather before slathering it on his face.

He grinned at his reflection, the white foam now covering the lower half of his face. Without the hairy beard, he knew, the scar left by the exploding cannonball would be visible from his chin to the outer corner of his right eye.

No matter. That scar, at least, was one he could wear proudly... unlike the grisly mess that was his foot.

Slowly, with each swipe of the sharp blade, James revealed another portion of the man he used to be. Gradually, a new confidence throbbed within. He could turn back the clock, he realized, provided he was willing to let go of his love—whiskey.

Love? he mused. *Hardly! More like hatred. Loathing. Revulsion.* James despised the amber liquid for its ability to dominate him, its control over every part of his life. Rather, what he loved was the power of whiskey to help him forget what he had become—a man who didn't deserve God's love, not to mention the love of a good woman like Joy McGuire.

But what was it she said to him on the subject not so many days ago? "None of us deserves His goodness, James. We're all sinners, but those who believe are forgiven sinners."

Another wisp of memory came to him then, something he learned as a child in Sunday school perhaps. *"Take therefore no thought for the morrow; for the morrow shall take thought for the things of itself. Sufficient unto the day is the evil thereof."*

So be it. He'd take one day at a time, as God instructed through that verse from the Good Book.

But just as James knew he'd be shaving his face every day for the rest of his life, he knew he'd also be facing the temptation to turn to the bottle every day. The war was not over. But at least he had the good sense to know that, alone, he didn't stand a chance against such a mighty foe. With God's help, he'd brace himself for the next battle....

❧

As part of his campaign to right his life, James decided to clean up the house, much as he cleaned up his face. First thing after breakfast, basking in the glow of Jeb and Missy's compliments on his clean-shaven new look, he headed for the attic, planning to start at the top of the mansion and work his way down.

He began by throwing open the tiny, rectangular dormer windows in the attic to let in the bright light and fresh air. Dust motes danced on sunbeams as he slid trunks and crates from beneath the cobwebbed beams overhead. Whistling merrily, he dug through box after box, sorting out the memorabilia of a lifetime. His mother's wedding dress would be properly cleaned and stored, but his threadbare baby clothes must be thrown away. His father's banjo would be re-strung, but his moth-eaten suit would have to be trashed.

He was up there nearly three hours when he came upon the strongbox, buried under several old quilts against the wall. James picked the lock with a rusting knife he discovered in the first trunk. Inside, in his father's familiar hand, James found dozens of letters and documents. The deed to Plumtree Orchards. The bill of sale for Abraham's first seed order. A love letter from his mother, written during the year of his parents' engagement. And a strange-looking package, sealed with wax and stamped with the Sheffield crest.

Curious, James broke the seal and slid the official-looking letter from its envelope.

Gentlemen, I write this letter with heavy heart and heavier mind, for here on this page I must admit what a coward I am, never to have claimed Jebbediah, son of Mary Claire, as my own flesh and blood. The boy, who now works as a stablehand, is, as of this writing, ten years and seven months of age.

That my dear sweet Ashley has been seriously ill these past twelve years is no excuse: I am an adulterer and a drunkard. Yet though I sinned against the Lord and my pure, innocent wife, God has brought a blessing in the form of a bright and

energetic man-child. It pains me that he now suffers a blot
upon his name because of my weaknesses.

The finder of this letter now knows the whole truth and bears
the responsibility of sharing that truth with Jebbediah. It is
my desire that the boy should inherit his rightful portion of all
that is mine.

On this nineteenth day of August in the one thousand eight
hundred and thirty-third year of our Lord, I remain sincerely,
Abraham Amos Sheffield

James's hands trembled as he reread the letter. Now he understood why, beneath Jeb's coffee-colored skin, the cut and angle of cheek and chin so strongly resembled his own. It explained, too, why Jeb's voice and smile reminded him of his father's. *Jeb is my half brother!*

His head whirled, the effect similar to the first dizzying swallows of whiskey. All these years since his brother George's death, James believed himself and Drewry to be the only Sheffields left on earth. To learn that he had blood kin, right here under this very roof, gave him an electrifying rush. He had a brother!

But how could he tell Jeb of his inheritance—one half of Plumtree Orchards—when James's neglect had all but destroyed it for both of them? The kindly, soft-spoken Jeb devoted his entire life to the place.

More importantly—and this thought brought a blush of shame to James's clean-shaven face—how could he now face this man, his blood brother, whom he belittled and ridiculed ever since returning from the War? Although he had always secretly liked Jeb and was pleasant enough to the older man in years past—except when he was drunk, of course—he considered Jeb a slave, after all, and treated him accordingly.

Sitting here under the weight of this news, James felt a powerful urge to hurry down the narrow attic steps and find something to ease his shame. Last week, long before his vow of abstinence, he hid a bottle of whiskey in the plant stand near the front door. If Missy hadn't watered the tree yet, it would still be there....

James stuffed the letter back into its yellowed envelope, folded it twice, and hid it in his pants pocket. *Just a sip or two to steady my nerves*, he told himself, *so I can think straight.*

He descended the stairs two at a time, stumbling in his haste to retrieve his stash. His palms were sweating as he lovingly wrapped his hands around the bottle's long, tapering neck and cradled it to his chest. Looking over his shoulder, lest someone see him with the bottle, James climbed the stairs to his room, slammed the door, and locked it behind him.

Suddenly, the air hung hotter and heavier than normal for a mid-August day. Breathing hard, James tore through the French doors and onto the balcony, and sucked in several lungs full of the humid air. When it did nothing to calm him, James held the bottle high.

Trembling violently, he uncorked it and brought it near his lips. His eyes watered as the pungent scent wafted into his nostrils. *Just one sip*, he repeated. *Once calm, I'll know what to do about the letter.*

The letter...

Written in his father's strong hand. The letter that told of Abraham Sheffield's addiction and what it cost his wife and Jeb and Plumtree. Judge Wilcox warned James that his behavior was dangerously like his father's. Would whiskey take hold of him until he, too, hurt everyone he held dear?

But that already happened, didn't it?

He treated Jeb and Missy shamefully. He let Plumtree crumble to near ruins. He sold nearly everything his dear mother ever treasured. His greed even drove his dear sweet Drewry from home.

It was like a vicious whirlwind—selling the family heirlooms to participate in high-stakes poker games, hoping to win enough loot to support his whiskey habit. Where would it all end?

His heart beat faster and his hair clung in damp clumps to his perspiring brow. Breathing heavily, he stared at the bottle in his hand. Comfort was right there, right there at the end of his arm.

Slowly, James tipped the bottle so that the mellow liquid touched his lips. His tears left ragged tracks down his cheeks, layered with the dust and grime of the attic. *Lord, give me strength*, he prayed.

"For the morrow shall take thought for the things of itself."

Where had that thought come from? He blinked and squinted, listening. No voice spoke the words, but he clearly heard them.

Uttering a loud, guttural cry, he yanked the bottle from his lips and hurled it from the balcony with all the power he possessed. It landed with a hollow clunk in the grass beyond the terrace.

His arms trembled as he leaned on the railing, his shoulders heaving with pent-up sobs. What gave him the courage to turn his back on whiskey's false promise of peace? Was it the answer to his silent prayer?

Just as Judge Wilcox said, he was walking in his father's footsteps. But James didn't want to live out the rest of his days, embarrassed by his every word and deed, banished to the outer fringes of polite society. He wanted to stand tall and proud once again. To be able to meet folks in the street and not feel inclined to look quickly away, too ashamed to meet the eyes of decent folk.

He wanted that more than anything. More, even, than whiskey. And, sad to say, there was only one way to accomplish his goal—abstinence—just as the judge ordered. No more sneaking sips of the brew when he thought no one was looking. No more pretending sobriety, when in reality, he teetered on the verge of drunkenness.

James knew exactly what he must to do.

He raced downstairs to find Jeb and Missy. "I can't explain it now," he said, handing Jeb the key to his bedchamber door, "but I want you to lock me in my room. Don't let me out, no matter what I say or do." With that, he grabbed a tin bucket, filled it with water from the kitchen pump, and headed back upstairs. "Search every nook and cranny of this house," he ordered as he went, "and destroy every bottle of whiskey you find. I don't want a trace of alcohol left on all of Plumtree when I next come down these stairs."

Jeb followed him into the foyer, and stood on the bottom step, the big brass key in his upturned palm. "You really gonna quit drinkin', Mistah James?"

James paused on the landing and turned to face his friend, his brother. He'd tell Jeb the whole truth, but not until he was in control of his life again. Then and only then could he hope to make the man believe his promise to right the wrongs he committed since coming home. "I'm gonna give it my best shot," he answered, a sad smile tugging at the corners of his mouth.

Missy pressed close to her husband's side. "We'll be prayin' for you, Mistah James."

James blinked back hot tears. "Thanks, Missy," he said, his voice wavering. "I can use those prayers."

With that, he went into his room and calmly closed the door behind him. He dumped some of the water from the bucket into the pottery pitcher on his dresser, putting the half-full bucket on the floor beside the French doors.

Footsteps sounded outside his door. The quiet click told James that Jeb did as he asked. James was locked in now...and the only way out was sobriety.

Glancing at the familiar surroundings around him, James unbuttoned his top button and rolled up his sleeves. He dipped up a handful of lukewarm water and sipped it, then lay back on his bed, and waited.

All his life, he heard stories down at the Silver Dollar about fellows who tried to go straight. They'd shake and sweat, curse and cry. Violent fits caused some to roll on the floor. Caused others, he heard, to bite off their own tongues as their bodies contorted in protest.

He closed his eyes and saw Joy's sweet face, heard her musical voice as he replayed the scene over and over in his mind: "We're all sinners," she said, "but were forgiven sinners."

James was afraid. More terrified than he'd ever been, even in the midst of that last bloody battle. But he was determined to face this enemy like a man, and win…or die trying.

EIGHT

It was Saturday, nearly lunchtime, but James would neither eat bread nor sip broth this day, for he was a prisoner.

His enemy was far more powerful than any he faced in Petersburg, and if he hoped to win the war against this foe, he'd have to do it, one agonizing battle at a time.

Faintly, through the thick oak door of his room, he heard the clock in the front hall begin to count the hours, *gong, gong, gong....* Though the clock was in the Sheffield family for generations, the notes of the giant timepiece struck no pleasant chord of remembrance in his mind. Instead, they rang hollow and empty, shaking him as surely as the cannon blasts shook him on that bloody Petersburg battlefield.

How symbolic that he chose this particular day...this particular time of day...to begin his fight for freedom, for in another moment, it would again be high noon.

In his agitated state, James couldn't help but think of his father. Abraham always enjoyed a good stiff drink. And why not? Initially, life presented him with many excuses: a bountiful harvest, the death of a loved one, the loss of a favorite pet, the birth of a child. With Abe, the list of good reasons to tip a bottle went on and on and on. Then, trivial things were worthy of celebration: finding a lost glove, learning that the cook baked a pie....

As the years passed, it became increasingly more difficult to distinguish the line between drinking to celebrate and drinking to forget. Abe's disposition changed from sweet to surly as quickly and as surely as the weather could change from calm to stormy. Once, Abe's foremost thoughts were of family and friends; thanks to alcohol, his major concerns revolved around where, when, and how he'd obtain his next drink. Because of his addiction the farm he single-handedly harrowed from the rocky northern Maryland soil would have gone to ruin. If not for his wife's persistence and his hired hands' devotion to her, Sheffield Estates would surely have died.

Hangovers turned James's father from a calm, jovial man into a raging madman who might disappear for days at a time, only to return, having completely blocked from his memory where he was, with whom, and what he did. These blackouts, like the hangovers, began happening with greater regularity and with greater intensity, until the day when James's mother, arms crossed resolutely over her chest, insisted that her husband choose: "It's me or the bottle, Abe."

James's father vowed to stop drinking then and there. And for a time, it seemed that his love for Ashley would win out over his love for whiskey. But the awful truth of the matter was that Abe simply learned to disguise his problem; eating licorice or swallowing pure lemon juice masked the telltale odors of his vile habit. Nearly a year passed before anyone realized he'd been drinking right along—in dark secret corners of the manor house, in the privacy of his library, in any one of the hundreds of stolen moments Abe carved from his days.

When James's mother realized the lie, she flew into a rage and banned whiskey from the house. But poor Ashley had no reputation for anger, never practicing fury as her husband had. Outraged that she came between him and his paramour, Abe lovingly carried his true love to the third floor of the Sheffield mansion where, in the lonely room overlooking the rose garden, he could caress the whiskey bottles as the golden contents crooned promises of everlasting faithfulness into his willing ears. It was there that Abe spent the remainder of his long, dark nights.

To all who looked on, it seemed that Abe might do anything for one more sip. And at last the man who was touted by all as one of the most honest in Maryland began to lie and steal and cheat to guarantee himself a steady supply of the poison that was slowly, steadily killing him.

Eventually, Abe began seeing things that weren't there. Ghastly beings, he insisted, that followed him from room to room, moaning and sighing as they threatened to pluck the very eyes from his head. Eerie, horrifying creatures that promised to cut out his tongue or smother the life out of him as he slept. His fearful shrieks could sometimes be heard in every dark corner of the big house, and the mournful cries haunted the boy James every bit as frighteningly as the ghosts haunted his father.

The demon alcohol had a gluttonous, ravenous appetite. After devouring his mind, it began eating away at Abe's body, too. His craving for whiskey overpowered his desire for anything nourishing. Soon, the big man who once stood straight-backed and proud shriveled away to a shadow. He shuffled through his fog-shrouded life like some toddler taking his first halting steps.

Even Abe's complexion changed from its former ruddy glow to a sickly pallor, and the clear blue eyes that once sparkled with wit and intelligence, reddened and watered behind drooping lids. Anger replaced his good humor; violence blotted out his gentle spirit. Sullen and withdrawn, Abe became unrecognizable to his sons and wife.

And then the unthinkable happened.

James was no more than nine or ten at the time. The sun was high in the sky on that sunny Saturday. He and his older brother just returned from a fishing jaunt, bamboo poles resting on their shoulders. They were laughing and chattering about the catch of the day—three bright sunfish and a colorful rainbow trout.

"They looked so sparkly and pretty in the water. What makes 'em fade once they're caught?" James asked George.

"Death, that's what," said the wiser older brother. "They're only beautiful while they're alive."

They spied Abe then, asleep on the porch swing, and clamped grimy hands over their mouths to still their high-spirited voices. Slowing their pace, they stepped carefully up the twelve brick steps that led from the flagstone walk to the wood-planked white porch. There they tried to blend into the shadows cast by the wide pillars slanting across the floorboards at their feet. Carefully, the boys tiptoed past their snoring father, knowing from painful experience that it would be dangerous to wake that sleeping monster.

Side by side and shoulder to shoulder, the brothers held their breath as they picked their way toward the front door. But despite their caution, a loose board creaked beneath their booted feet as they tried to sneak by his slumbering form. Had it been George's footfall or James's that pierced the pleasant, peaceful afternoon? The boys would never know. But even if they each lived two lifetimes, they'd never forget what happened next.

Abraham leapt from the porch swing as though propelled by a gigantic catapult, flinging arms and fists and curses with equal abandon. Like a wild beast, he charged them, murder and mayhem in his bloodshot eyes as he swayed to and fro in a drunken stupor. "I'm your father," he bellowed, "and I deserve your respect!" With each step, Abraham's voice grew louder and more maniacal.

His sons shrank back in soundless fear.

"You'll show me respect, confound you, if I have to beat it into you!"

The threat of harm to her youngsters brought Ashley to the door. "What's going on?" his wife wanted to know in a tremulous voice.

Without bothering to acknowledge her with so much as a sidelong glance, Abe thundered, "I'm about to teach these unruly young'uns of yours some manners!" He shook his fists in the air. "To do the job you, as their mother, should have done, and teach them how good sons should behave around their father!"

Hands clasped at her throat, Ashley's face blanched. "Come inside, boys," she whispered, and though she managed to hide the tremor in her voice, there was little she could do to mask her fear. "It's time to wash up for lunch anyway...."

Abe blocked their path, chest heaving as he stood there, glowering like a mad dog. "They'll have no lunch," he hissed through clenched teeth. "They'll go hungry, that's what they'll do, for waking me and reminding me what a miserable couple of blots on my life they are!"

He held his head in his hands and grimaced. "They've given me a headache the size of Virginia!" he moaned. Then, without another word of warning, he started for them again, rolling up his sleeves as he went. "I'll teach you some proper manners if it's the last thing I ever do!" he said again, eyes slitted, lips taut. "This'll be the last time you wake me from a dead sleep, tell you that much!"

James and George looked around for a way out, but seeing no possibility of escape, flattened themselves against the porch rail. And very much as he did that day on the bloody battlefield, little-boy James cried, "Please, Daddy, don't beat us again...."

Abe turned a deaf ear to his younger son's pleas. And as he staggered toward them, his eyes, now rheumy with a whiskey haze, blazed with raw hatred for his offspring.

The boys closed their eyes and gritted their teeth, waiting for the blows to fall—young hands clamped over their ears to blot out the sounds of his feet, tramping closer, closer; bony shoulders hunched to their earlobes as they cringed at his approach. But both boys were tempted to peek when they heard a strange cracking sound that suddenly split the air.

Later, alone in their room, George would whisper, "I thought it was Daddy, breaking your arm...." In the next moments, they learned it wasn't a bone shattering at all. It was, instead, the sound of splintering wood.

Abe propelled himself toward his sons with such force that he hadn't been able to stop once he actually reached them. Though he lost at least fifty pounds, he was still a man of considerable bulk, and that bulk crashed through the porch rail as if it was constructed of brittle rock candy rather than sturdy pine.

When James and George opened their eyes, the first person they saw was Ashley, standing just inside the door, mouth agape, eyes wide with fright. Following her disbelieving gaze, they turned in time to see Abe falling, falling, for what seemed an eternity before landing with a dull thud.

Mother and sons huddled together at the edge of the porch in the jagged opening Abe's body opened in the once-protective balustrade, and stared in humbled silence at his body, twisted and still amid the bright red azalea blossoms.

As the big grandfather clock in the hall began to strike the hours—gong—they waited for some sign that he survived the fall, but Abe didn't blink.

Gong...

They inspected his chest closely, but it did not rise, did not fall.

Gong...

They held their breath, wondering if he'd flick a finger.

Gong...

Or twitch a toe.

Even as the clock struck twelve, Abe remained motionless.

"Drink killed your father," Ashley whispered, pulling her boys into the protective circle of her embrace. "Don't ever give whiskey a chance to kill you, too, my sweet sons."

James took a deep breath and willed the awful scene from his mind. But it was no use. The ugly memory refused to leave him. He glanced around his room, dim because he closed and locked the French doors and shut out all sunlight by pulling the deep-green velvet curtains together. Fitting and proper that darkness should shroud him like a moody black cloak, he mused.

"Don't let drink kill you," his mother said. Without knowing it, Judge Wilcox echoed her words during his recent visit. "Drink killed your father," his old friend said, "just as it'll kill you, if you don't look out, my boy...."

Drink killed him, and it'll kill you.... Drink killed him and it'll kill you.... Drink killed him and...

James let out a loud sigh, drew his feather pillow to his chest, and bit down hard on a corner of the embroidered pillowslip. He locked himself in this room, knowing full well that he was fighting for his life. What if he lost the battle? What if he chose to cling to the bottle instead of clinging to a possible future with Joy?

He'd lose Plumtree, his newfound brother, any hope of reconciliation with Drewry....

A life without Plumtree would be shameful.

Life without Jeb, bleak indeed.

But life without Joy...

How could he face another dawn without the prospect of spending the rest of his life with her?

A sob ached in his throat as he rasped, "Lord God Almighty, don't desert me now."

No sooner had he uttered the words than a wracking pain coursed through him. It began in the pit of his stomach and gripped him, tighter than the vise in the toolshed ever gripped wood or steel, and held James with a fierce relentlessness. He brought his knees to his chest and hugged them to him.

This is only the beginning, James realized. The pain tearing at him now was only a small sampling of what he could expect before his torment knew a final and welcome end. It might take hours, he knew, days, even, before he walked from this room, victorious over Whiskey.

"Lord God Almighty," he sobbed out, "give me the strength to see it through...."

⌣

The clock in the downstairs hall struck the last muffled note of twelve. He was in this room for twenty-four hours.

Drenched with sweat and tangled in the damp sheets, James laid in a tight ball in the center of the bed. His head ached. His ears were ringing. His hands hurt from clenching his fists. He was bruised and bleeding from beating the walls. He was tired and thirsty and hungry.

But he wasn't drunk.

And he wasn't drinking.

Best of all, he didn't crave so much as a sip of whiskey at the moment. That, at least, gave him hope.

He sat up, slowly, and waited for the spinning in his head to subside. Running his tongue over his dry lips, he remembered the water he poured into the pitcher when he began his solitary vigil a day ago. Dropping first one foot, then the other, over the side of the bed, James tested his strength. Holding onto the mattress for support, he put his weight onto his wobbly legs. Amazingly, they carried him to the dresser, where he hoisted the pitcher in trembling hands and lifted it, slowly, to his lips. The warm water did little to quench his thirst. But it was wet and soothed his parched throat.

He never tasted anything more glorious in his life. He poured a bit of it into the bowl beneath the pitcher, placed the pitcher beside it. Then, leaning over onto the dresser with one quivering arm, he dipped the other hand into the liquid and ran it over his stubbled chin and through his tousled, perspiration-soaked hair.

Sometime during his night-long ordeal, he'd torn the shirt right off his back. It lay in a tattered heap in front of the French doors. James picked it up, swaying a bit when he bent over, and hung it on the bedpost. He rested there for a long moment and looked slowly around the room.

Shards of glass sparkled in the corner near his mahogany chiffonier. Before his personal battle began, it was a cut crystal vase that Abe gave Ashley for their first anniversary. Fragments of white plaster of Paris littered the floor near the door. Until now, that was a lovely hinged box, in which Ashley kept the ruby ear-bobs Abe gave her on her thirtieth birthday.

These knickknacks reminded him that the whole house was once filled with such mementos, both his brother's and his parents'. But that was before James's habit drove him to sell the articles, piece by memorable piece, to pay for yet another bottle to quench his insatiable thirst.

When his brother George and his wife were killed, and James learned that George willed Plumtree Orchards to him, his heart swelled with pride. His big brother entrusted him, not only with the running of the plantation he built out of fields of rocks and grit, but with the care and nurture of his beloved daughter, Drewry.

And James readily accepted the challenge.

His first major decision as head of Plumtree Orchards was to turn his father's manor house on the hill into a place where any guest would feel welcome—not that he had many overnight guests in recent years. That feat gave him great satisfaction, for James always preferred his brother's happy house to his father's. Some of his fondest memories, in fact, were made in the sunny rooms that George built. More importantly, he knew that remaining at

Plumtree, where Drewry lived those first years of her young life, would be best for his orphaned niece.

Now, surveying the results of his destructiveness, James straightened and lifted his chin a bit. *That's all part of the past now*, he told himself. *The first test is the hardest, and you survived it.* Setting his jaw, he strode over to the French doors and opened the curtains wide, threw open the doors, and sucked in a lungful of cleansing air.

He passed the first test. He *passed* the first test!

A weary smile on his face, James turned abruptly and began stripping the bed of the soiled sheets. Then, using the remnants of his shirt, he brushed the bits of glass and plaster into a tidy pile and tossed the whole mess into the fireplace. Rooting through the chiffonier, he found a clean pair of trousers and a starched white shirt. He'd wash and shave, then wait for Jeb or Missy to check on him. They'd been pacing the hall outside his room, like sentries guarding a gold mine, nearly every hour on the hour.

Won't they be surprised when they return, to find that I'm in control of my life at long last? Something bubbled inside him that he hadn't felt in a long, long time. Such a long time, in fact, that he was forced to search his memory for a name to put to the feelings.

James's smile widened when at last he came up with a definition for the emotions churning happily within his heart...pride and gratitude.

⌒

"I always thought you an' me looked an awful lot alike," Jeb said, grinning, "'specially 'round the eyes." His own dark eyes crinkled with pleasure. "So, we is brothers!" He shook his head and sighed. "Reckon that's why Abe was always so good to me...."

The two men sat side by side on one of the hard stone benches that flanked the terrace. With identical motions, each leaned his elbows on his knees, folded his hands between them, and stared at some invisible spot between his feet.

James nodded and shifted uncomfortably on the bench. "He went to his grave carrying that awful secret inside of him." He stared straight ahead for a long, silent moment, remembering first the loving father Abe had been, then the drunken bum he became; first the affectionate man who dispensed bear hugs, then the violent beast who doled out cruel punishments. James's mouth formed a tight line. "May the Lord have mercy on his soul."

Though he hadn't spoken aloud his warring thoughts, Jeb nodded, too, for he'd been victim of that seesawing spirit that had, for so long, controlled their father.

"You've been like a brother all my life, though I only recently discovered it," James admitted. "You stood by me, no matter what." He shook his head. "You rightfully own half of Sheffield Estates, but I'm ashamed to admit it's not worth what it could have been if I hadn't…"

Jeb held up a silencing hand. "This ain't no time to be beatin' yourself up. What's done is done. What do you say we don't look back to what's past, and look ahead to what's gonna be?"

James turned slightly and met the chocolate brown eyes of his half-brother. What kind of man was this, who put others before himself? "I can't hide Drewry in the past," he said, his voice a harsh whisper. "If I hadn't driven her away, she'd be so happy to know that you're her…"

"…my niece," Jeb said, his voice rough-edged as he attempted to stifle a sob.

James smiled slightly as his blue eyes dimmed. "I sorely miss that young woman. If I knew how to contact her, I'd tell her how very sorry I am for all the misery I've brought her."

Jeb cleared his throat and stood. Pocketing both hands, he began to pace. Suddenly, he stopped in front of James. "You ain't brought her no misery."

James's brow furrowed in confusion.

"I know where Drewry's been all these months."

James was on his feet now. "How could you know?"

Jeb sighed. "Got a confession of my own. Somethin' I been aim in' to tell you for some time now." Shrugging, he added, "Never seemed to be the right time somehow...."

James understood all too well what Jeb meant. There was never a time when he hadn't been too drunk, or too hung over, or too furious about being in the chasm between. Grimacing, he gritted his teeth and sat on the bench again, turning to meet Jeb's gaze. "Tell me. Where is she?"

Folding both arms over his chest, Jeb planted his feet a shoulder's width apart. Raising his chin slightly, he stared at James, as if considering the foolhardiness of telling such a truth to a man who so recently was locked into a room, fighting the aftereffects of twenty-four hours without whiskey. As he studied his newfound brother, his eyes softened and he smiled. Joining James on the bench once more, he said, "She's on a purty li'l plantation just outside o' Richmond. 'Magnolia Grange,' I b'lieve it's called."

James measured his words carefully, for he was indeed angry. But his wrath was self-directed. He knew full well why Jeb wasn't able to tell him where his...their...beloved niece went. "You've been corresponding?"

Jeb nodded. "Real reg'lar-like. A letter ever' couple o' weeks."

"She's all right, then? She's safe and happy?"

Jeb studied his younger brother's face, and satisfied the questions were rooted in genuine caring and concern, said, "Some trouble now and again, but nothin' our Drewry can't handle." He snickered.

"Stood up to a Klansman, she did."

James grinned. He could almost picture her, petite and feminine, nose to naval with a strapping bully, unafraid—or so she'd make it seem—of his threats. "That's our Drew-girl, all right."

Then, after a moment, his smile faded. "I need to talk to her, Jeb. I need to set things straight." He grabbed the older man's shoulders and shook him gently. "Will you write and ask her if she'll see me?"

Jeb frowned. "You come through the night right well," he said, admiration and respect shining in his dark eyes, "but it's a mite soon to be traipsing' off to Richmond, ain't it? I mean, what if... what would ya do if..."

"If she sends me packing?" James rose to pace back and forth, then stopped in front of Jeb. "It would be no more than I deserve," he admitted. "But at least I'll have tried. I have to right the wrongs I committed, Jeb. How else can I regain control of my life?"

Sucking in a long breath, Jeb shrugged and nodded. "Don't reckon you can set things right, less'n you see 'er eye to eye." He paused, then got to his feet and headed into the house.

"Wait," James called after him. "Where are you going?"

Jeb stopped, then said over his shoulder. "I do believe I got me a letter to write."

NINE

James would catch the ten o'clock train out of Freetown, Jeb told Joy on his last trip into town. The man had no sooner spoken the words than she decided to be there to meet James at the station. She gave him a proper send-off, too, so he knew that at least one person would be looking forward to his return.

Twenty miles separated Plumtree from town, and as she sat on the wooden bench beside the station doors, Joy watched the horizon. Her heartbeat quickened each time she spied a wagon, a coach, a man on horseback; it slowed when, on closer inspection, she realized the oncoming riders were not James Sheffield.

Finally, she spotted him, and a tiny gasp of pleasure escaped her lips as his familiar form drew near. Jeb sat beside him on the buckboard, but James held the reins. Wasn't it just like him to do the work other plantation owners relegated to their employees?

As he drew the team to a halt, Jeb sent her a jaunty wink. She hadn't told James's hired hand of her plan, yet the mischievous glint in his eyes told her he wasn't the least bit surprised to find her there.

And James…He'd shaved his thick, dark beard, Joy noticed right away. Quite a change. Quite a nice change.

She stood as he leapt down from the wagon. Stepped closer as Jeb handed him a boxy brown leather valise. "Have yo'self a safe trip," Jeb said. "And give Drewry my best regards when you see her, y'heah?"

"I'll do that," James answered. "Take care," he added, gripping Jeb's hand in a meaningful handshake.

Something was different between these two, Joy noticed. A new bond connected them, the intensity of that bond almost palpable.

James climbed the three wooden steps onto the platform and stomped road dust from his boots. "It's good to see you," he said, tipping his hat as she approached. "And what might you be doing here?"

Dare she tell him she was there to see him safely off, that she pried the schedule of his departure from Jeb? What would he think if she admitted she plunked herself down on that bench nearly half an hour ago? Ignoring his question, she cocked her head. "You've shaved your beard. I must say you look quite distinguished without it. But when did you make that decision?"

Running a hand across his broad chin, James laughed softly. "Couple of days ago. Guess I needed a change…."

Joy gave the bag a cursory glance. "Looks like you'll be staying wherever you're going for quite a while."

He set the valise on the platform and gazed down into her eyes. "I'm going to Richmond—" he squared his shoulders "—to visit my niece."

Joy nodded. He told her about Drewry, and she knew how much this trip must mean to him. His excitement at the prospect of seeing his niece again after so many months of separation was visible in his bright blue eyes. She never saw him happier—or more nervous. Joy sent a silent prayer heavenward that the visit would be everything he wanted it to be.

"About the beard," he began, interrupting her prayer, "I shaved it because I needed to make a whole new start. It's part of the new me."

Joy arched a brow in mute puzzlement.

"I've given your words a lot of thought…about the power of choice, I mean." He took her hand. "I've given up whiskey, once and for all."

Both brows disappeared behind her bangs now. Joy placed her free hand atop his. "Oh, James," she whispered, "that's wonderful!"

Bright patches of crimson flooded his cheeks at her compliment. "I'm not foolish enough to believe I'll not be tempted again, but I've made the decision to quit, at least." *Before I become another Abe*, he added mentally.

James proceeded to tell Joy how he sequestered himself in his room, with the help of Jeb and Missy, to fight the first round of whiskey-related battles. With each word, it seemed, her delight increased the width of her smile.

"I've seen enough to know you'll succeed, James. It won't be easy, but you can do it. I know you can!"

He wanted to take her in his arms on the spot and show her how much her encouragement meant to him. Without it, he knew, he'd never have summoned the courage to take that first step. He wanted to thank her for her faith in him. Instead, James took a deep breath and began telling her how he planned to come clean with Drewry. Joy nodded and smiled, looking prettier than any woman had a right to.

He might have stood there for hours, talking to Joy, if the train hadn't rumbled into the station at that moment, hissing and steaming and making it impossible to hear or be heard. Might be standing there still, instead of sitting in the passenger coach, seeing none of the scenery that whizzed by as he stared out the window, hearing nothing of the clattering of train wheels against iron rails, not to mention the low hum of his fellow passengers' conversation.

All he could see was Joy's face. He heard her musical laughter. Felt her warmth all around him, like a comforting mother's hug. And he carried her last words to him in his heart for a long, long time. "I believe in you, James," she said as he stepped onto the train. "Hurry back now, because I'll miss you."

⌐⌐⌐

Until now, Joy kept her feelings for James to herself. To admit that she loved him would be spiritual suicide at this point. James needed her strength, her patience, her there-when-he-needed-it guidance, not the willy-nilly giggles of a schoolgirl-like crush.

The longer she knew James—the better she knew him—the more Joy realized she was in danger of falling helplessly in love with him. His warmth and generosity were contagious, his quick wit and sense of humor utterly charming. He seemed to know exactly what to say and do, and exactly when to say and do it.

But then, she only saw him drunk once....

She shared her fears with Red Shirt's wife the very afternoon of James's departure. "You refrain from judging others," Running Deer said, "yet you harshly judge yourself. Do you not have the same right to find happiness as everyone else?"

Joy vowed on her eighteenth birthday—the day she became, in her own mind, a woman—that her life belonged to the Lord. To dream of romantic love, a husband, children seemed selfish indeed.

"You have traded your future happiness for the happiness you believe your mother would have known, had she lived." The Indian paused. "You seem to forget that Ruth chose whiskey over you, over your father, over God in heaven. Even if she had seen one hundred summers," the dark-skinned woman went on, "she would not have spent a truly happy moment on this earth."

Joy opened her mouth to protest, but Running Deer lifted a graceful hand. "In your heart, Laughing Eyes, you know it is so. In your mind, you believe what I say." The touch of her fingers against Joy's cheek was feather light. "Even as a young girl, you knew...that your mother died long before the river ended her life."

Joy's eyes brimmed with unshed tears. Yes, she acknowledged the futility of her mother's recovery. Ruth never wanted to recover. "But through God," she said, clinging to His promise that hope is everlasting, "all things are possible."

Running Deer shook her head. "Your faith is indeed strong. It was Ruth whose faith faltered...and failed."

She hugged her young friend. "But you did not come here today to speak of the past, did you, Laughing Eyes?" With a knowing wink, the Indian woman went on, "You came here to speak of what is in your heart for the sad-eyed one."

Joy nodded. For a long time now, she and Running Deer and Gray Hawk had shared this secret name for James. And it was true; a certain sadness haunted the clear blue gaze. "I know he's trying, but I wonder..."

"...if he will stumble?"

Joy let out a long sigh and turned to watch some children playing tag.

"Your real worry is not that he will fall, for you believe he has enough faith to see him through this trial...." Running Deer looked up from her weaving to fix Joy with an unwavering stare. "You yearn for his love, yet you fear you are unworthy of it."

Joy's head spun. How could this woman read her heart? Oh, yes, she felt unworthy. Hadn't she let her own mother down when she needed her most? Joy's self-centeredness had cost Ruth her life!

"Before we have known many winters," Running Deer continued, weaving a turquoise thread in and out as skillfully as she was weaving a picture with her words, "we have no understanding of time. It stretches before us like the lands beyond, and to our eager young eyes, it appears to go on forever." The Indian woman paused, searching Joy's face. "Vows are like that, Laughing Eyes, for we make them long before we understand the permanency of them."

The pulse in Joy's throat fluttered. What was Running Deer trying to tell her, that the promise she made as a young girl—the promise that became the vow of a young woman—was born of immaturity and naiveté? And therefore, worthless?

Though Joy had not spoken her thoughts, Running Deer nodded. "God knows your heart, Laughing Eyes. He knows why you made such a promise; perhaps He would not hold you account-able to it for a lifetime."

Joy ran that possibility round and round in her mind. The echo of it left a certainty, where before, only questions circled like vultures. That certainty now brought a peace she had not known in years—not since her eighteenth summer.

⌒

James's jangled nerves cried out for release. Just one sip of whiskey.... He'd have even settled for the port wine served in the richly appointed dining car. But a small voice—little more than a whisper—warned him to avoid all temptation. Joy believed in him. He couldn't let her down.

Besides, abstinence was the key. Everyone said so. Now, if only he could abstain from temptation....

To distract himself from the ever present possibility, James struck up a friendly conversation with the couple at the table across the way. Their idle chatter temporarily served to keep his mind from his yearning. Then, when the waiter took his order and brought out his steak and potatoes, he applied himself to the excel-lent meal.

But he was not prepared for the goblet of sherry that followed....

"Compliments of the chef," the waiter told him with a conspiratorial wink.

James never took his eyes from the glass. "Thank you," he rasped, his throat suddenly dry. The waiter nodded and placed a small plate of biscuits and a tiny tin of butter on the table, and then he was gone.

James inhaled the delicate aroma, wafting from the goblet where it squatted in the middle of the table. His mouth began to water. He licked his lips and swallowed hard as one hand inched slowly closer to the snifter. A fingertip—as if it had a mind of its own—flicked out and wrapped around the cut-glass stem. It would take very little effort now to slide the container toward him, lift it to his lips, and quench this unquenchable thirst.

He held the glass lovingly, then caressed the rounded contours with thumb and forefinger. Tilted it right and left, watching as the thick, syrupy stuff stuck, momentarily, to the inside of the snifter, then slid, ever so slowly to the center.

Heart racing, James's hands began to tremble. He thought he left the worst of the shakes behind that long harrowing night, locked in his room. Thought he left the sweats behind, too, a week later, when his need for a drink drove him to the point of despair. Again, he insisted that Jeb and Missy bolt him into his bedchamber. He beat back the demon on both frightening occasions. But the experiences only served as vivid reminders that, at best, he'd only be allowed to hold the monster at bay. Never, he realized would he truly conquer this beast.

Closing his eyes, James sent a fervent plea heavenward. *Give me strength, Lord. Help me turn from temptation.*

When he opened his eyes, James took a last, longing look at the snifter's contents. And then, without hesitation, he slid it back where the waiter left it. He would not move it out of reach. Nor would he ask the white-coated attendant to take it away. He exercised some self-control, that's what! Nothing could make him drain that glass as he longed to do.

Nothing but weakness.…

He fished in his pocket and drew out his watch. It dangled and spun at the end of a sparkling gold chain until he clasped it tightly in his palm and pressed the pad of his thumb against the knob. With a quiet click, the lid sprung open, and James read the black Roman numerals on its silver-white face. He'd arrive in Richmond in two hours, providing no farmer's cow wandered onto the tracks and slowed the train's steady progress. An hour after that, and he'd be in the company of his beloved niece. How could he go to her reeking of alcohol when he assured her, time and again, in the letter that preceded this trip, that he gave up the wicked stuff, once and for all?

With quiet deliberation, James buttered his biscuit and took a huge bite. Its sweet-and-salty texture tingled against his palate. He followed it up with a chunk of the steak, then a forkful of potato. Hard as he tried not to, he found himself staring at the shimmering drink that still sat there, mocking him.

And then, from the other side of the car, where several businessmen were laughing and talking, one held a bottle of whiskey high in the air. "Join us," he called to James, "in toasting our good fortune."

James had just taken another bite of steak when the invitation was made. His jaw froze in response. The gentleman repeated his offer, extending the bottle of whiskey. "We've just sealed a sweetheart of a deal. Help us celebrate our joy!"

Joy.… Her smiling face floated in his memory as James licked his lips, then took the starched white napkin from his lap and dabbed his sweat-slick forehead. He hoped no one could see the violent trembling of his hands.

"Now, look-a here," the businessman persisted, "it ain't ever' day I invite a total stranger to share my luck. What's the problem, man? You a teetotaler or somethin'?"

Drawing a deep breath, James pushed his chair away from the table, then stood in the aisle between their tables. "I mean no offense," he began, dropping his napkin onto the seat of his chair, "because I genuinely appreciate the friendly gesture. Not too long ago, I'd have emptied your bottle single-handedly by now." He grinned and nodded toward the whiskey. "But I've got important business in Richmond. Can't afford to arrive for this meeting with liquor on my breath."

"Your loss," said one with a shrug of resignation.

With that, the men resumed their hearty laughter, dismissing James to return to his seat in the passenger car. There he began counting the minutes until he'd see his beloved Drewry once more.

❧

The moment he arrived in Richmond's Chesterfield Hotel, James handed the concierge a twenty-dollar bill. "I need a quiet room where my privacy will be assured," he told the stunned young man.

Like the money crumpled in the boy's hand, James's train ticket and the meal he would buy Drewry came from the sale of his mother's piano. He was far from proud of the fact. This time, unlike other times he traded goods for cash, James felt not a burning guilt, but a stirring of hope. Rather than whiskey, this money would ensure a happier future for Drewry...and for himself.

On the train he vowed to set about turning Plumtree Orchards into a productive plantation the moment he returned home. For now, however, he had more important business—righting the wrongs he did his niece.

He settled in the hushed parlor and focused on the double doors, hidden behind heavy red velvet drapes. James glanced again at his pocket watch. Any minute now, she would be arriving...he hoped.

Would she still be as lovely and innocent as ever? Or would she have been ravaged by the life she was forced to lead because of his greed? Had she been safe? Happy? He reminded himself that Jeb was corresponding with Drewry, and that, according to her letters, she would soon wed a certain Chase Auburn of Richmond. Maybe her dark eyes would gleam with at least a spark of the admiration she once felt for her uncle. Or would she be angry still? Could she ever forgive him for what he did to her?

Just then the doors swung open. His heartbeat quickened at the sound of it. A bellboy in a gold-trimmed red uniform held the thick tasseled curtain aside, then tipped his brimless cap as Drewry stepped over the threshold. Ignoring all ladylike reserve, she flew into her uncle's outstretched arms.

"My precious Drew-girl," he whispered into her ear. How long since he spoke those words? Two years? Five? Drink clouded his memory. "Thank the good Lord you're here. I was afraid you'd change your mind."

Drewry pulled away, far enough to look into his face and touch his smooth cheek. "Now, why would I do that, Uncle James, when I've looked forward to seeing you for weeks?"

Tears shimmered in his sky-blue eyes. "Thank you, Drewry," he said softly, "for loving me…still."

"You've shaved your beard," she noted, her eyes sparkling. "My, but don't you look handsome. And at least ten years younger than the last time I saw you!"

James tipped his head back and laughed. "It's part of my new image."

Drewry's laughter blended with his as an elderly waiter stepped into the parlor. "Tea is served," he said stiffly, smoothing the white napkin that rested on the black sleeve of his waist-length jacket.

"Shall we?" James asked, offering Drewry his arm. "We'll toast forgiveness with tea and crumpets."

She giggled at his crude imitation of the man's British accent.

They were shown to a small, round table near the window of their private room. The delicacy of the lace tablecloth, the gleam of the silver, the translucence of the fine china—none of this compared with the beauty sitting across from him.

"I've so much to confess," he said, passing her the silver tray.

"No need for that," she said, helping herself to one of the tiny cucumber sandwiches arranged on the lace doily.

He held up a hand to silence her. "Oh, but there is, if I'm to make things right." He took a deep breath. "There are certain… deceptions…."

"Deceptions?"

James put down the tray and steepled his hands. Taking a long breath, he focused on her lovely face. "I'm not the war hero you think I am."

Drewry fiddled with the embroidered trim of her napkin as she stared, wide-eyed, and waited for him to continue.

"If they gave medals for cowardice, I'd have a whole collection." He exhaled a deep, shuddering breath, then told her how he earned the scars on his face, how he "earned" his limp. He couldn't meet her eyes and his voice dropped in desperation as he confessed, "The Yankees didn't shoot off my foot. I did…to get out of fighting another day."

There was a long pause. Then Drewry reached across the table and placed her hand over his. "No wonder you turned to drink. But no one needs to know, Uncle. One mistake doesn't alter the fact that you'll always be a hero in my eyes."

The compassion in her expression threatened to undo his determination to continue. How like her to say something warm and reassuring, despite the months of discomfort she endured because of him. How like her to put his needs ahead of her own.

He inspected the even features, the porcelain complexion. Yes, she was still the same loving child who ran away all those months ago rather than suffer his cruel treatment.

But something had changed. She carried herself with a new assurance. Spoke with a new confidence. Sometime during the years he was drowning his own sorrows in drink, his little Drew-girl became a woman.

James knew he'd never live long enough to make up for all the wrongs he did her, but he would treat her with respect and admiration from this day forward. "Thank you, Drewry, for your kind words, though I don't deserve them. What drove me to drink," he explained, "were the dying words of one of my men who…saw what I did." James gazed into space, as if looking into some unspeakable horror.

"With his last breath, he gasped out, 'How could you…?'"

"I'm sorry for all you've suffered," Drewry said. "But God is merciful. I'm sure He's forgiven you."

James's answering smile was tinged with remorse and sadness. "God is indeed merciful. He sent a messenger of His mercy in the form of Joy McGuire, my beautiful Indian princess."

At Drewry's insistence, he told her how he met Joy on the banks of the Gunpowder and told her everything that followed. Told her that if he could believe for one moment she'd have him, he'd ask Joy McGuire to marry him. And that, thanks to Jeb, the whole mess with Porter Hopkins was a thing of the past.

Before James could lapse into further self-blame, Drewry quickly sketched in the facts about her own life since they had last met. How she met the widowed Chase Auburn and his two adorable, motherless children. How they already weathered several crises together at Magnolia Grange. She told her uncle that if Chase would only ask her, she'd be his wife.

"He's an imbecile if he doesn't ask!" James injected. "Why, he'd have the sweetest, most loving wife in the whole state!"

"And if Joy turns you down, she doesn't deserve her name!" Drewry countered.

They shared a moment of quiet laughter, allowing the healing moment to carry them back to happier days. "So you forgive me, then?" he asked.

She hesitated, and for a moment, James feared she might refuse. Then Drewry jumped to her feet and flew around the table to his side. "How could I not forgive you? You're my Uncle James!"

The words, like a warm blanket, comforted him all the way home.

TEN

James had been back from Richmond for no more than half an hour when he saddled the big black mare and headed into town under the pretense of buying sugar for Missy's kitchen. Knowing that Joy routinely headed home from the schoolhouse at precisely three o'clock every afternoon, James carefully timed his exit from the store to coincide with her passing.

His heart swelled at the sight of her. The light in her eyes and her sunny smile told him that her parting words were sincere. She had missed him.

The moment he caught up with her, she said it again. "It's been lonely around here without you, James."

James fumbled with his own thoughts as he limped along beside Joy on the dirt road that led from Freetown to the Suscataway village. Should he tell her he thought of little else but her since leaving?

"Why not thank the Lord properly, and come to church with me on Sunday?" she suggested when he told her how well his visit with Drewry went.

James chuckled. "It's been so long since I've been inside a church, the stained glass windows would most likely fall out of the panes if I stepped across the threshold."

Joy grinned. "If that's your excuse for staying away, it's a feeble one, and you know it. The Bible is very clear on the issue, James," she added, wagging her finger under his nose. "We're to keep the Sabbath holy."

He read the teasing glint in her eyes, which widened in pretended shock when he playfully grabbed her extended finger. *For you*, he thought, *I'd even endure one of Matthew Frost's long-winded sermons*. Frost's reputation for fire-and-brimstone lectures spread through Freetown like a plague. Folks endured them, James surmised, because they felt duty-bound to do so. He had no such inclination, yet for Joy…

Suddenly, the arrogant young preacher's boast—that he was Joy's intended—was more than James could stomach. He told Drewry as much, and she wondered if such a thing were only wishful thinking on Matthew's part. "Why don't you ask her yourself?" his niece suggested. "A woman appreciates a man who considers her opinions and feelings."

James cast Joy a sidelong look. "Will Matthew be giving the sermon this Sunday?"

"You're in luck. Father is in town." She stifled a merry giggle, clapping her hand over her mouth. "Matthew only conducts services when my father is out of town."

But it wasn't Matthew's preaching that concerned James. "Have you and Frost been…friends…for very long?" he asked carefully.

"I've known him for several years. Whether I'd call him a friend…" She shrugged. "Well, I suppose I don't know him all that well. He rarely talks about himself. But then, we can't hold the man's serious nature against him, now can we? He works very hard, and I'm sure he's quite sincere."

James's spirits took a downward turn. Why was she defending the miserable minister? he wondered. Why was she trying to convince him of Frost's worth...unless she considered him husband material?

And what woman wouldn't? Matthew was an educated man who earned a decent salary. Owned his own home—modest, but comfortable. Someday, he'd have his own parish, too, and when he did, he'd have a bigger paycheck, a bigger house to offer his wife.

Matthew was also a respected citizen of the town. Clean-cut and decent, without as much as a blemish on his sterling reputation. A man with both feet planted firmly on the ground. James grinned sardonically. *Whereas one of my feet is firmly planted in the ground!*

There was nothing amusing, however, in James's final thought: Matthew Frost was everything James Sheffield was not.

⤳

Throughout the Sunday service, James felt Matthew's cold green gaze assessing him. James shifted uneasily on the hard wooden pew as he held the hymnal for Joy. Having her near helped distract him from the young assistant pastor's glare. Hearing her sweet voice, lifted in song, inspired him to try a few of the old favorites himself. Long-forgotten melodies awakened in his memory, and James found himself belting out the beloved lyrics as if he'd been a faithful churchgoer all his life. Heaven seemed very near—beside him, in fact, he thought, as he stole a glance at Joy's radiant profile.

But all it took to bring him back to earth was a quick glance in Matthew's direction. Self-doubts resurfaced. Self-recriminations rang louder, even, than old Mrs. Henderson's rendition of "Amazing Grace" on the harpsichord. Who did he think he was, sitting here in God's house beside an angel? How dare the town drunk presume to win the heart of this fine, upstanding young woman!

At that moment Joy caught his eye, her clear soprano carrying the familiar message to his heart: "that saved a wretch like me. I once was lost, but now I'm found...." And he felt a surge of hope, despite the icy glare Matthew cast in his direction.

And then Pastor Samuel McGuire came to the pulpit to begin his sermon. He spoke of Christian charity. Kindness and acceptance. Forgiveness. "You cannot forgive those who trespass against you," declared the white-bearded man with an air of authority, "unless you first forgive yourself." His blue eyes locked with James's.

It was as if Joy's father read his mind. James sat up straighter in the pew.

"Put aside self-doubt and self-loathing, and take up the shield of God's love and mercy."

James felt Joy's elbow in his ribs, and when he glanced at her, he saw the slight tilt of her lips. "Pay attention," she whispered.

He was beginning to relax, basking in an unfamiliar sensation of peace, when he saw again Matthew's frosty stare. James dropped his head and studied his folded hands. Admittedly, he was a lout, a liar, a cheat, and a low-life drunkard. But he wasn't that man any more. He gave up whiskey; successfully turned from the temptation to take a drink half a dozen times since making his initial vow; endured the agonizing sweats and tremors that accompanied purging his body of the poison.

This time, when Matthew's green gaze sought him out, he didn't look away. Instead, James lifted his chin and squared his shoulders. He was a new man. A better man. Whether or not his new "self" deserved a woman so fine as Joy McGuire remained to be seen. But, James decided, there in the sunlit interior of St. John's church, what man did deserve her? Certainly not the likes of Matthew Frost!

Joy's hand, resting on James's sleeve, stirred him from his reverie. "Josh McClintock usually takes up the collection," she said softly, "but he's in Baltimore, visiting his folks. Would you mind helping out today?"

He wouldn't have denied her anything, least of all such a simple request. He followed her whispered instructions to the letter, taking the brass bowl from the marble-topped table in the back of the church, handing it to the person sitting nearest the aisle, then waiting for it to make its way back to the end of the next row. Copper pennies, nickels, and shiny dimes clinked against the plate.

When he collected the offering, James dropped in a silver dollar. Things weren't good at Plumtree, but they were better than they were in years, and God was at the center of the positive changes. Then, at Joy's direction, he took the bowl of money to Samuel's office, put it on the good pastor's desk, and covered it with a white altar cloth.

"I'm thankful for your assistance, son," Samuel said, heartily thumping James on the back when the service ended. "I do believe the sight of you with the collection plate in your hand inspired the good folk of Freetown to give more liberally than usual."

James could not resist a wink and a chuckle. "If the town drunk can reform, God's power is mighty indeed, eh?"

"Will you join us for Sunday supper?" Joy asked. "Deer steaks, mashed potatoes, gravy, green beans…"

"…and Joy's famous deep-dish apple pie," Samuel added. "I'm thinkin' you'd be wise to take 'er up on the invitation."

"Then how could I refuse? Just tell me when I should arrive."

"Come along with us now," Joy urged. "I need a hand peeling the potatoes."

James hadn't peeled potatoes since he was a boy. But the prospect of performing the lowly household chore at Joy's side was incentive enough to—

Suddenly, Matthew's excited voice disturbed the amiable atmosphere of worshippers who lingered to visit after the service. "Attention, everyone!" he shouted. "We have an emergency situation on our hands."

All conversation halted abruptly, with only a few murmured questions rippling through the room as the group gathered closer, awaiting an explanation.

"Someone has stolen today's collection," Matthew said as he leveled an accusing gaze on James. "The thief even took the bowl!"

James turned to Joy, to explain that he did exactly as she instructed, to assure her that he hadn't taken a cent of the collection, that he even added a silver dollar of his own....

She was staring, openmouthed, at Matthew. But what James now saw in her stricken face froze the blood in his veins. Could she possibly believe that he stole the money?

ELEVEN

Why, James groaned inwardly, had he let Joy talk him into coming to church after he was away for so many years? And as if that were not enough, she wrangled him into passing around the collection plate, too. Now he was in a real pickle.

The good people of Freetown thought James took the money. And why not? Most of them knew he sold nearly every stick of furniture in his house to pay for drink. If they hadn't personally purchased his family heirlooms, they knew someone who did.

He liked to think he never sank so low as to steal from the church, even if he hadn't reformed. But James was in sad shape—almost as bad as his father before him. He never stolen anything, but even James couldn't be sure he might not have—if caught between a rock and a hard place. A man who gambled away his beloved niece for whiskey was capable of anything.

So the moment he heard the money was missing, he expected the pointed fingers, the whispered speculations. James didn't even bother to defend himself. Instead, he climbed on his big black stallion and rode home. If they dug up some kind of false proof of his guilt, he'd go willingly with the sheriff and suffer the consequences, living on the fringes of proper society. In the meantime, he waited out this latest tempest, praying all the while that the good Lord would see fit to clear his name.

What the others thought of him didn't matter. He lived under the dark scowls of their disapproval for years, and it hadn't killed him yet. What Joy thought of him, however, mattered more than he cared to admit. If she no longer believed in him, how could he continue fighting this lifelong battle?

He knew the moment she began doubting his innocence. He saw the suspicion skitter across her lovely features just before she composed herself. Still, momentarily, her eyes darkened with the same fear and revulsion he saw there when, in a drunken stupor, he stumbled against her on the boardwalk and knocked her to the ground.

With Jeb and Missy in Pennsylvania visiting one of Missy's ailing relatives, James was utterly alone in the big Plumtree mansion. He paced the floors, each footfall echoing hollowly through the empty rooms. Although the temptation to take a drink was almost overpowering, he resisted stubbornly. One sip and he'd ruin his record of nearly a hundred days without a single drop of whiskey.

A hundred days liquor-free, despite the fact that for years, he stashed the stuff throughout the house. But why should he be without it when he needed it most, he thought, his resolve wavering? Maybe there was a bottle still hidden away in some nook or cranny....

If they were so all-fired determined to accuse him, he may as well be guilty of some crime! James ranted mentally.

Like a gigantic magnet, the hidden liquor tugged at him. Following his instincts, he located a bottle in the butler's pantry, hidden in the dumbwaiter; one in the buffet drawer, and another behind a row of books in the library. He could hole up here for days before his supply ran out. By then, maybe he'd remember where he hid another bottle, and another....

James lined up the bottles on the mantel in his bedchamber. Like little soldiers, they stood at attention. They never let him down, or wrongly accuse him, or misjudge him.

"Guilty is as guilty does," he chanted as he poured a golden stream of whiskey into a sparkling, cut-crystal goblet. He held out the glass, turning it this way and that as it reflected the bright rays of the afternoon light. James brought the mouth of the glass under his nose, closed his eyes, and inhaled deeply of its strong bouquet. His mouth watered.

"This is your future," Red Shirt warned, pointing out the village outcasts. "Take a good look at how you'll live your life until God calls you home."

Remembering, James's hands began to shake, and he set the glass on the table beside his wing backed chair. It mocked him silently as he pictured the dirty, disease-ridden men who would spend their last days just out of reach of those they once held dear. He remembered the stench of them, wandering aimlessly from place to place within the confines of the little camp on the outskirts of the Suscataway village. They may as well have been lepers, for all the attention paid them.

"Is this the way you want it?" Red Shirt had probed. James moaned. He'd rather be dead.

But then, he admitted with resignation, if he took a single drop of whiskey in that glass beside him, he was as good as dead right now. He began to tremble at the thought.

Weeks ago, James found the family Bible on one of the library's dusty shelves. He rubbed linseed oil into its leather cover and let the nearly translucent pages fall open at will. "*There hath no temptation taken you but such as is common to man,*" he had read, "*but God is faithful, who will not suffer you to be tempted above that ye are able; but will with the temptation also make a way to escape, that ye may be able to bear it."* First Corinthians 10:13 became James's credo on that day, and he'd been reciting it ever since.

He recited it now, first silently, then aloud, and waited for God to show him an "escape." The grandfather clock near the door chimed three times. He'd been alone for nearly three hours with all this whiskey so near, yet he hadn't given in to the yearning for a swallow of it.

Suddenly, James knew what he had to do. Without a moment's hesitation, he rose from the chair, gathered the whiskey bottles from the mantel, and carried them outside. Then one by one, he uncorked and upended them, allowing the contents to gurgle out onto the ground.

James stood back and stared for a long moment at the empty bottles littering the ground. He hadn't won this battle for Joy, he realized; nor for Jeb or Missy or Drewry, for that matter. No, he did this for himself, and no one else.

It felt good, very good indeed. And though he single-handedly sidestepped the temptress, whiskey, yet again, James knew who was responsible for bringing him safely through. One name resounded in his head. One alone could be credited with his conquest—the Lord God. James's heart thundered with the pure joy of His might and glory.

James picked up the empty bottles and brought them inside, doubting that whiskey would ever have the power to hurt him again. Let the sheriff come and arrest him for stealing the church's money, he thought. When the deputies came, at least they'd find him sane and sober.

He rinsed the bottles and stood them on the kitchen windowsill. Maybe Missy could use them as vases for her chrysanthemums....

Then, smiling, James saddled his horse and headed for the Suscataway village, where he'd share with Red Shirt this small but significant victory.

Halfway down the river road, James met up with the sheriff and his deputy. "Hold up there, Sheffield," the older man said. "I've got a few questions for you."

James was expecting this; the only surprise was that it hadn't come sooner. "Fire away, Sheriff."

"I understand you attended Sunday services this morning."

James frowned. "Let's save ourselves a heap of time, sheriff. You want to know if I stole the money from the collection plate, and the answer, quite simply, is no. I've been a drunkard and a gambler, and I've been down on my luck, but I've never been a thief."

The sheriff removed his black derby and scratched his balding head. "Judge Wilcox wanted me to ask you straight out. Said you were an honorable man, and that if you took the money, you'd own up to it.

The judge said that about me? A glimmer of hope sparked within James. If a man like Orlando Wilcox believed in him, then maybe in time, the rest of them could learn to trust him…

"I know what you're thinking," James offered. "I'll go quietly if…"

"No need for that." The sheriff met James's level gaze. "I'm just doin' my duty, you understand, and questionin' possible suspects is part of it."

He didn't needed to spell it out. James knew exactly who headed the "Get James" committee. The only question now was what Matthew Frost would do next. "Then I'm free to go?"

The deputy cleared his throat. "Law says we gotta warn you to stay close to home. Weren't all that much money taken, but that ain't the point. It's the…it's the…"

"…the principle of the thing," James came to his rescue.

"You been spendin' lots of time out at the Indian village," the deputy continued. "They's good people, them Suscataways. It's God's work you been doin', teach 'em to cipher an' such."

James smiled and silently praised the Lord. Already, he showed James that one's old life could be forgotten, could be replaced with a clean, untarnished one. "I enjoy the few hours I'm able to get out there. Takes my mind off my own troubles."

The deputy nodded. "Had me a brother who fell victim to liquor," he admitted simply. "Broke my poor mama's heart to watch him kill himself, one wicked ounce at a time."

The sheriff cleared his throat. "Well, now, we best be on our way, Jenkins." To James, he said, "For what it's worth, Sheffield, I believe you. You've been drunk and disorderly more times than I can count, but I'd bet my last dollar you'd never stoop so low as to steal from the church."

For a moment, James wished he still wore his thick beard, for it might have hidden the flush of embarrassment the sheriff's compliment brought to his face. "Thanks, Sheriff."

"No thanks necessary, Sheffield. I'm just old and grizzled enough to know that most times, a man earns the attitudes folks hold about him." With that, he turned his horse around. The deputy followed, and then they were gone.

James took the low road that ran alongside the Suscataway village. More than ever, he wanted to share his good news with his friend, Red Shirt.

The Indian greeted James as he hitched his horse to a tree. "This is a new man I see before me," he observed, sweeping James with an assessing glance. "I barely recognized you without hair on your face."

Standing taller, Red Shirt lifted his head to gaze into James's face. "I see peace in your eyes. You have passed a test since last we spoke?"

James nodded. Riding out from Plumtree to the village, he thought he might tell his friend all about it, step by slow and painful step. But standing sure and strong beside his friend, James found he had no need of Red Shirt's approval. It was enough that God was pleased.

Red Shirt placed a bronzed hand on James's shoulder, his black hair glistening in the sunlight. "You have traveled far in a short time. It is a good sign."

The two men walked together through the center of the village, where women busied themselves over stewpots and children played nearby. Life, for the first time since the battle at Petersburg, seemed full of promise for the future.

It would have been a blessing, James thought, to share his new life with Joy. Sadly, that would likely never happen. What she thought of him was written all over her pretty face when Matthew announced that the church money was missing. Even without that episode to create suspicion in her mind, he doubted he had a chance with her. After all, she belonged to his accuser, Matthew Frost. And although it distressed him thoroughly, James knew he'd have to relinquish.

While he loved Joy—yes, he could admit it now, if only to himself—he was resigned to living without her for the rest of his life. It was part of the punishment he'd have to bear for his sins.

TWELVE

James awoke, squinting into the bright sunlight that poured through the open French doors and slanted across his face. Throwing the sheets aside, he sat up.

Today he'd right the wrong that Matthew Frost had done him. James hadn't taken a cent of the church money. But someone had. Who? The answer that kept running through his brain was always the same—Matthew Frost himself!

Yes, he'd confront the assistant pastor, high and mighty as he was, and demand a confession. And if Frost wouldn't admit what he did, James would beat it out of him.

He leapt from his bed and dressed carefully. After shaving, James combed his hair into place, then knotted a string tie at his throat. It was important that he look his best, for it wasn't every day, after all, that the town drunk accused a minister of theft.

Shortly before noon, James arrived in town. No sooner had he delivered his horse to the livery than he spied Matthew, heading in the direction of his small cottage behind the church. James waited until the assistant pastor put his hand on the doorknob.

"Frost," he said, stepping onto the boardwalk, "I want a word with you."

Matthew's tawny head turned in the direction of the menacing voice. Surprise, then disgust, scuttled across his features as he recognized James. "Brother Sheffield," he said, his gaze narrowing, "have you something to confess?"

"No. But I believe you have."

Matthew cleared his throat. Confusion, tinged with genuine fear, replaced his arrogant smirk. "I'm sure I have no idea what you're talking about, Brother Sheffield. Perhaps we should step into the pastor's office, where we can discuss your concerns privately...."

James crossed his arms over his chest. "Nope," he said firmly. "Since I have nothing to hide, I'm staying right here, in plain sight of the good folks of Freetown."

The minister bit his bottom lip. "I've work to do, Sheffield—important work. So, if you don't mind...."

Planting his boots apart, as though rooted to the spot, James grinned. "I'll get to the point, Frost. Rumor has it I skipped town and rode all the way into Baltimore to get liquored up on the money I stole from St. John's. And the gossips are saying the story originated with you." He punctuated his statement by poking his forefinger into Matthew's chest.

The assistant pastor loosened his tie and shifted his weight from one foot to the other. His Adam's apple bobbed up and down as he tugged at his collar again. "There must be some mistake. Gossip is a sin, you know."

"And lying is a sin, too. Stealing, a bigger one yet." Matthew's lips thinned to a taut slit.

James took a step closer, and stood—almost nose to nose—with Matthew. "Where are your manners, man? Aren't you going to invite me in? Offer me a cool drink of water, perhaps?"

Matthew grabbed a handful of James's shirt just as the Widow Hanson passed by. "Why, Pastor Frost," she said as Matthew quickly unhanded James, "your face is beet red, and you're sweatin' bullets. You'd better get in out of this hot sun, before you keel over!"

Frost whipped a starched white hanky from his breast pocket and mopped his brow. Forcing an amiable grin, he gave the widow a courteous bow. "I assure you I'm quite well. But I thank you kindly for your concern."

"Good day, Pastor, Mr. Sheffield." She nodded. Then, almost as an afterthought, she winked at James and whispered, "I do declare. You were a handsome man when you were bearded and drunk. But now that you've left both behind, you're liable to attract a downright stampede of eligible females!" She turned and walked away, her coy laughter trailing behind.

Overhearing, Matthew bristled.

"Open the door, Frost, and invite me in," James insisted. "Unless you're hiding something in there."

Matthew's blush deepened as he struggled to maintain eye contact. "Of course I've nothing to hide. It's just that I'm not very handy with a mop and broom, you understand, and things are... shall we say...a bit disheveled."

"Open the door," James repeated through clenched teeth, "or I'll open it for you."

Matthew relented, but blocked the doorway. "At least let me clear a chair for you first."

"I'm not stayin' long enough to sit," James barked, pushing past Matthew. He tugged at the string on the window shade, then stood back as it snapped upward, flapping at the top of the frame. Looking around, James turned to face the preacher. "Why, Matthew, you're a fine housekeeper. I don't believe I've ever seen a tidier room. You could bounce a coin off that bed," he said, nodding toward the narrow cot against the wall.

He turned just in time to see the young pastor's wide green eyes, darting from James to a cupboard near the window. James opened the first door. "Neat as a pin," he said, inspecting its contents, then opened another door. "Mmmm. Cleanliness is next to godliness, eh, Matthew?"

As James reached for the last door handle, Matthew rushed forward. James never saw the doubled fist coming, and it landed on his cheek with a painful whack, sending him sprawling onto the floor. He scrambled quickly to his feet and effectively blocked the next blow.

"Get out of my house," Matthew ordered, "before I call the sheriff and have you arrested for trespassing."

Rubbing his cheek, James laughed. "Trespassing? But, Matthew, you invited me inside. Even the Widow Hanson heard you. Has the heat gotten to you, man?"

Matthew rushed him again, but this time James stopped him with a hard fist that landed square on the young minister's narrow nose. While he lay dazed near the door, James opened the last cupboard door and peered inside. "My, my, my, what have we here?" He withdrew the cloth-covered brass collection plate, still brimming with Freetowners' coins. "How do you suppose this got in here?"

Matthew's cheeks were now a chalky white. He sat on the floor, dabbing his bloodied nose with the hanky.

"I...I...It...um..."

"You disgust me, Frost," James said quietly as he stepped over the pastor's body and out the door.

Although Matthew appeared momentarily stunned, the sight of James hurrying toward Samuel's office, revived him. "Brother Sheffield!" he called. "Come back here! You don't understand. It's a mistake, a terrible mistake."

Ignoring the man's entreaties, James knocked on Samuel's closed door. "Reverend!" he hollered. "Reverend McGuire!"

"Wait!" Matthew shouted, running up beside James, panting from exertion. "Don't do this, James. I can explain...."

The door opened and Samuel's bearded face, at first smiling and happy, took on a somber frown. "James! Matthew!" he demanded as if scolding two unruly boys. "What's going on here?"

Joy stepped up behind her father, and her eyes widened at the sight of the blood pouring from Matthew's nose. "You've been fighting?" she asked, incredulous.

"All right, get in here," Samuel ordered sternly, "and start explaining."

"I…I caught him. I…uh…caught him redhanded," Matthew stammered. "He broke into my place, no doubt trying to return his ill-gotten gain…trying to make me look like the guilty party!"

James's first instinct was to clobber the man again. But one glance in Joy's direction stopped him cold. There, on her lovely face was that same disappointment he saw when Matthew announced that the money was missing. "It's not true, Joy," he hastened to say. "It—the collection plate—was in his kitchen cupboard…."

A crowd gathered outside the open door. "What's up?" asked one man. "Fight," answered another. "Who's fightin'?" someone else wanted to know. "Matthew Frost and James Sheffield," called a fourth.

"It's over the collection money," said a woman in a loud whisper. "Matthew says James was tryin' to put it back and frame him for stealin' it!"

"You don't say!" her lady friend shot back.

The Widow Hanson faced them all. "You're all a pack of rumormongers. Give the poor man a chance to prove he's left his old life behind. How do you know he's taken to drinkin' again after his brief reform? And what proof is there that he stole the collection money?"

"Enough!" Samuel bellowed. "Go home, all of you, and pray the Lord will show us the truth."

Silence descended, and the crowd dispersed, drifting in clusters to their homes.

In all that while, Joy stood still as a statue, hands over her mouth, looking first at Matthew, then at James, and back again.

"I can't prove that what I say is true," James began, "but I didn't take the money. I found it in his cupboard," he turned to Matthew, "right beside the silver dollar."

"What silver dollar?" Matthew gasped.

"The one in the collection plate, where I put it yesterday during the service."

"You put a whole dollar in the plate?" Joy squeaked. "And you say it's still in Matthew's cabinet?" Samuel wanted to know.

"He's lying!" Matthew shouted, red-faced. "He's lying because he's in love with Joy. He knows she's my intended, but he wants her for himself. He'll do anything to blacken me in her eyes."

Samuel faced James. "Is this true? Do you love my daughter?"

James was pretty sure the answer was written all over his face. Unflinching, he turned to meet Joy's wide-eyed gaze. "I can't deny that I love your daughter, Reverend. But I didn't steal the money. It's just as I said…I found it in Matthew's cupboard."

Samuel nodded soberly. "I believe you, me boy."

James's pulse quickened. Had he heard correctly? The man of God actually believed him?

"I saw it there with me own eyes, just this morning," Samuel explained, "when I stopped by to ask if young Frost saw my fountain pen. The pen was never missing, mind you, but I had my suspicions about the incident." He aimed an accusing glare at Matthew.

"You closed the cupboard door mighty quick, son, but not quick enough. I was hopin' you'd see the error of your ways… and come to me with the truth before…"

James's heart sank. So the good reverend hadn't believed him, after all. If he hadn't seen the money for himself, he'd probably still believe Matthew.

The assistant pastor, meanwhile, was struggling to control his emotions. "All right! I admit it! I took the money! But I only did it because I love her, too," he said, swallowing a sob. "I thought if I could show her, once and for all, that Sheffield is a no-good scoundrel..."

Seeing the look of disdain on Samuel's face, Matthew broke off and took a new tack. "I never intended to keep it, sir. I'm no thief! I only thought..."

Joy's eyes filled with tears. With a look of pure agony on her face, she glanced at each of the three men in turn, then fled from the room.

⇛

Joy didn't stop until she reached Running Deer's hut. She barged inside and found her friend seated on the floor, sewing beads on a pair of her son's moccasins. "Laughing Eyes, won't you come in?" the Indian teased.

But Joy was in no mood for jokes. "Matthew took the money and tried to make it look like James did it!" she burst out. "They both say they love me, but each one is trying to protect me from the other." Joy's practiced control dwindled. "Oh, Running Deer, I'm so confused!"

The Indian woman's gentle smile further softened her pretty features. "What confuses you, Laughing Eyes? It seems very simple to me. Which man has won your heart?"

Joy blinked back her tears. "James. I love James."

"Then I do not understand your confusion, my friend."

Joy sighed. "I'm ashamed to admit it, but for a while, I thought maybe James took the money. I was afraid he gave in to temptation and needed the money for..."

"...for whiskey?"

Joy nodded miserably. "Oh, Running Deer, how can I say I love him when I don't even trust him as I should?"

The woman stared off into the distance and spoke with wisdom beyond her years. "Trust is something one must earn, not something handed over like a gift. In time, he will earn your trust. Until then...simply love him."

THIRTEEN

Joy moved through the village with the grace of a deer, stopping now and then to chat with the women or watch the children at play. For half an hour or so, she watched James, the center of attention in a spirited game of lacrosse. Despite his limp, he managed to maneuver the hard little ball from place to place by catching, then flipping it with the netted end of his stick.

He was quick and agile, and laughed whether he made a good play or a bad one. Though most of the boys in the game were only half his age, James managed to keep pace with their intensity and speed. The game ended with good-natured backslapping and a hearty shaking of hands.

~

Not until he tucked in his white shirt did James realize who was observing him from a distance. Flushed as much from the awareness of his pretty spectator as from his intense activity in the early autumn heat, he brushed his hair back from his sweaty face and strolled over to greet her.

"Sorry you had to see our team lose," he told Joy with a sheepish grin. "That display ought to hold you for months."

"On the contrary, it was fascinating to watch you play."

"Fascinating? You take delight in witnessing a grown man make a fool of himself?"

She returned his playful smile. "You held your own...considering you were the oldest player on either team."

James faked a frown. "Now wait just a minute. You don't think I limped all the way over here to be insulted, do you?"

His grin was contagious. "Why did you limp over here, then?" she asked, tilting her head flirtatiously.

"The truth?" he asked, suddenly serious. "I couldn't have stayed away if they offered to pay me."

For a long moment, Joy and James stood stock-still, eyes fused in a soul-stirring meeting. Joy's cheeks flushed as deeply as James's, though she participated in no recent physical activity.

How could she have ever suspected him of stealing the collection money? A man with such a clear, honest gaze couldn't possibly be a thief! She admitted weeks ago how much she enjoyed his company; admitted more recently how much she enjoyed the man himself. Now Joy was reluctant for the moment to end.

"I put a rabbit in the stewpot before I left," she said, searching for a way to prolong their visit, "with potatoes and carrots and parsnips. Will you share a meal with Father and me?"

James arched a dark brow. "You're inviting me to supper with the pastor and his beautiful daughter? Why, what will the good people of Freetown think if they see you consorting with a known drunkard—one who is suspected of robbery, at that?"

Joy shifted uneasily. "What the good people of Freetown think is of no concern to me," she retorted.

James lowered his voice. "But what about your intended?"

She blinked in confusion. "My...intended? What intended? I'm not, nor have I ever been, promised in marriage."

Nodding, James smiled slightly. "I had a notion the betrothal was more a figment of his imagination than fact."

"What are you babbling about, James Sheffield? Whose figment are we discussing, anyway?" Sparks of anger flashed in her eyes as Joy narrowed her lips in frustration.

"Raises your dander a mite not to be believed, doesn't it?" he asked, reminding her that she, too, entertained suspicions about him.

She flushed with embarrassment, but ignored the comment. "Well, what are you waiting for? Are you going to tell me who I'm to marry, or not! I have a right to know who I'll be spending the rest of my life with, don't you think?"

James chuckled at the forcefulness emanating from the petite frame. "Matthew seems to be suffering from the delusion that he's to be your husband in the very near future. He alluded to the fact that Samuel handpicked him from a long line of suitors."

Joy stamped a black-booted foot. "Well, I never!" she hissed. "When I get my hands on that man...."

"In all fairness to Matthew, who can blame him?"

At that, Joy who had been pacing back and forth, arms crossed over her chest, muttering under her breath, halted abruptly and swiveled to face James. "What did you say? I don't understand."

"I said...that any man would be proud to claim you as his bride."

Her anger vanished as quickly as it rose. If the eyes were the mirrors of the soul, as Shakespeare wrote, the true James Sheffield was pure and decent indeed. And he cared deeply for her. That much was evident on his handsome face—that rugged, battle-scarred face. "You look so different without the beard. Did I tell you how much I like the change?"

Again, his quiet chuckle warmed the space between them. He stroked his clean-shaven chin. "There's nothing to hide behind now. Guess I have no choice but to walk the straight and narrow."

Joy reached up and touched his cheek, letting her fingertips linger there, relishing the gentle rasp of stubble that began forming. "The beard hid nothing, James Sheffield. I saw you for who you were…almost from the beginning."

It took every ounce of self-control he could muster to resist pulling her into his arms. He loved this tiny bundle of energy, although he could never subject her to a man like himself. She deserved only the best, and the good Lord knew the best wasn't James Sheffield.

Perhaps life with Joy would soften Matthew Frost, James mused. He learned how forgiving the people of Freetown could be, for they extended the hand of friendship and forgiveness once they learned what Matthew tried to do to James. It seemed their kindness had somewhat thawed the icy young pastor. Perhaps Joy could teach him to smile more often, to give and receive love….

James blinked away the vision of her, dressed in wedding finery. Why couldn't he be the man in the morning coat who stood beside her at the altar, rather than the arrogant Matthew Frost? Why couldn't James take the vows to love and to cherish, to protect and to provide, to comfort and care for Joy all the days of her life?

He took a deep breath. *If it's meant to be*, he thought, *the Lord will show me a way….*

"Well," Joy was saying as she smoothed her dress, "shall I set another place for supper?"

James smiled regretfully. "Much as I'd like to, I think it best to decline. Matthew made a good point when he said your reputation could be tarnished by your association with me."

Again she stamped her foot. "Matthew has no right to judge you, nor has he any right to dictate who my friends will be! You will eat with us," she demanded. "If it were possible, I'd set up a table in the town square. I'm proud to be your friend, James Sheffield, and I don't care who knows it!"

In a great surge of emotion, he drew her to him and held her tight. "And I'm proud to be your friend, too," he whispered into her darkly shining hair. *Ah, my dearest Joy, but I'd like to be so much more than just a friend. If you knew me as you think you know me...*

It was time to come clean with Joy, to expose his darkest secrets. If she harbored no ill will for him after hearing all the dirty truths that made up his past, perhaps there was hope for them, after all. If not, he'd salve his conscience with the knowledge that he was upright and honest, despite the cost. Certainly that would be worth something as he stood before the great white throne on judgment day!

James held her at arm's length, then took her hand. "Walk with me," he said. "I have something to tell you."

She said nothing, but went along willingly.

In the shade of a weeping willow, he invited her to sit beside him on a smooth boulder. "You say you saw me for who I was, even when my beard hid this hideous scar," he began. "But there are things about me that you must know...if we're to continue being friends."

Joy sat patiently, waiting for James to bare his soul. And bare it, he did. He left nothing out. Not the way he played dead on the battlefield or nearly blown off his own foot to escape further combat. And though he already told Joy what he did to his niece, just for good measure, he reminded her. And he didn't have to tell her about his former attitude toward his servant, Jeb—his newly found half brother! "I want all my cards on the table," he explained, "so there's no mistaking who I really am."

She sat in stunned silence for what seemed to James an eternity, staring at her hands, clasped tightly in her lap. Joy made several attempts to speak, but no words passed her parted lips. He wouldn't rush her, one way or the other. Whatever she decided, he would learn to live with it.

As he waited for her to say something—anything—James closed his eyes and prayed...with *"the temptation, also make a way to escape, that I may be able to hear it."* He took solace in God's promise and drew new strength from it, for even if Joy said she never wanted to see him again, he'd always have the Lord to see him through.

Suddenly, without warning, Joy stood. Then, looking him squarely in the eye, she issued a crisp ultimatum. "Supper is at five o'clock sharp. Don't be late...or you'll have to make do with a cold dinner."

With that, she marched off. She hadn't gone ten feet when she stopped, turned, and added, "And for goodness sake, please don't wear a tie!"

James and Joy were together nearly every day after that. With Joy's help and encouragement, Plumtree Orchards took on a semblance, at least, of its former grandeur. By selling off a section of bottomland, James was able to buy enough paint to coat every trim board on the big brick mansion, and to purchase new furniture to fill the empty rooms. Newly curtained and carpeted, the place, once again, was home.

The change in James himself was even more remarkable, he supposed. Without the poison of whiskey flowing constantly in his veins, his eyes brightened, his skin took on a healthy glow, and his dark hair glistened. There was a bounce to his step, despite his limp, and there was energy—and to spare—for all the chores he assigned himself around the place.

When the invitation to Drewry's wedding arrived, it seemed perfectly natural to ask Joy to accompany him to Magnolia Grange. Mindful of propriety, James asked Little Crow to ride along with them. Never having been aboard a passenger train, the child's enthusiasm was contagious, and the three laughed all the way to Richmond.

Drewry had not exaggerated the splendor of Chase Auburn's stately southern plantation, James decided upon arrival. Auburn land stretched as far as the eye could see in all directions. How Magnolia Grange had been spared by the Yankees was anybody's guess, but James sent a silent prayer of thanks heavenward that its beauty remained untouched.

He half expected Auburn to send a servant to welcome them or, at best, to greet him with detached civility. The man was well aware that James gambled his niece away in a drunken poker game. So James was prepared for whatever treatment Auburn might deem appropriate under the circumstances. In place of a cold reception, however, the trio was warmly greeted.

～

The two days prior to the wedding were a flurry of activity. Joy volunteered to decorate the mansion with wide white satin streamers and lavish arrangements of flowers. Then she helped the household staff prepare for the hundreds of invited guests. James pitched in by setting up the neat rows of chairs in Auburn's charming outdoor chapel where the wedding would take place. He scaled the trout and butterfly-sliced venison Chase's cook would serve at the reception.

On the morning of the wedding, the family gathered around the breakfast table and prayed that the warm weather would hold through the day. Temperatures in the seventies, even in Richmond, were unheard of in December. *But leave it to Drewry to ask for the impossible, and get it,* James thought fondly.

It was with pride that he marched down the white-carpeted aisle with his beautiful niece on his arm. In the church vestibule earlier, trembling with happiness and excitement, she gave him a big hug. A sob choked off the words in his throat. How could he tell her how much he loved her, how sorry he was for all the pain he caused her?

Now, as they strode toward the altar where her handsome husband-to-be waited, gratitude flooded James. His beloved Drewry forgave him—even found happiness in spite of it. Upon returning to Plumtree Orchards, Jeb and Missy would begin building a lovely home of their own, just a mile down the road from the old mansion. James whipped the whiskey monster (at least, he held it at bay for many months). He turned the house back into a home again, and in just a few months, he would begin working on the next season's fruit crops. Best of all, Joy hadn't rejected him, not even when she learned every ugly detail of his past.

Life was good, and James gave thanks.

Sitting in the rough-hewn pew beside Joy as Pastor Tillman performed the marriage ceremony, James made a life-altering decision. Perhaps it was inspired by the pomp and pageantry of the wedding vows, or being surrounded by loved ones, or even the glorious spring weather that warmed this winter day. But whatever its source, James only knew that before this day ended, he would ask Joy to be his bride.

～

The journey back to Baltimore seemed to take far longer than the trip to Richmond. None of the laughter and banter, the anticipation, the gay chatter that hurried the trip south was heard as they traveled north again.

James always prided himself on being a man who thought things out; who planned ahead; who considered all sides to an issue before taking action. At least, that's the kind of man he was before the War…and since attacking his alcohol problem. So then, why—when he formulated the marriage proposal in his mind—had he failed to consider the possibility that Joy might say no?

James's grief was raw and real, no doubt visible for all the passengers to see. Besides, there was no point in hiding his sorrow and disappointment. He worked long and hard, after all, to turn his life around. He struggled valiantly these many months to become a worthwhile human being again. Why had he done it, if not to make himself worthy of Joy McGuire?

He went over and over it in his mind, from the moment he dropped to one knee and took her tiny hand in his, looked deep into the beautiful, velvet-brown eyes, and whispered hoarsely, "Miss Naomi Joy McGuire, will you do me the honor of becoming my bride?"

She blinked in surprise. Swallowed once, twice. Her hand in his stiffened as she replied, "I can't, James." With that, she snatched back her hand, lifted the billowing blue satin skirt of her gown, and raced across the lawn to hide in her well-appointed room.

Hours later, Auburn's scullery maid found James, still down on one knee, just as he was when Joy left him. "Is there anything I can do for you, sir?" she asked in her lilting Irish accent. Dumbly, he shook his head. "I know it's very forward of me to say this, sir, but you're pale as a ghost. I just want you to know that I'll not leave you here alone. I'll make a pest o' meself if I must to see you get inside, safe an' sound. It's gettin' dark, and you'll catch your death out here."

She tugged at his arm until he stood, then led him back to the house, chattering non-stop about what a lovely wedding it was and what a beautiful bride Drewry made. "My name is Bridget, sir. Bridget McKenna. If you need anything," she said as she left him outside his door, "just ring for me."

As he listened to the rattle of the train, James realized he never even bothered to thank the young woman for her kindness. Perhaps, when he returned to Plumtree, he'd write her a brief note…

He glanced across the aisle, where Joy sat woodenly, staring as the Virginia landscape raced past the window. Little Crow, sensing that all was not right between his two favorite adults, fidgeted nervously on the seat beside her.

If only she gave him a reason, maybe his heart wouldn't ache so. It would be better, so much better, if she told him why she wouldn't marry him. Any excuse she might have given would have been better than the awful possibilities rolling round in his head at this moment.

"Your true test is yet to come," Red Shirt said in reply to James's boast that he drained three bottles of whiskey—over the terrace wall. He hadn't understood the Indian's warning at the time, but he understood it now.

Joy was his test! If he could learn to live whiskey-free—without her, he'd be free of alcohol's grip forever!

FOURTEEN

That James had been avoiding her was patently obvious, Joy mused. Once, when he saw her walking down Main Street, he crossed to the other side, pretending not to have seen her at all! Several days later, as she waited in line to pay for a bag of flour and a sack of dried beans at the general store, James stepped up behind her. The moment he realized who was standing right in front of him, he left his purchases on the counter and marched out without a word.

This nonsense went on entirely too long, Joy decided. She'd confront him today—no two ways about it! Life without him was admittedly bleak and devoid of pleasure. *I DO love him*, she told herself. *And he loves me, too. He admitted it in front of half the town, and he asked me to marry him!*

Joy recalled the pained expression her refusal etched on James's handsome face. She hated having to turn him down without as much as a by-your-leave. But she couldn't tell James that her father objected to him—any more than she could explain she'd never marry anyone without her father's full blessing. She was an obedient, dutiful daughter all her life. And no man, not even James Sheffield, was worth Samuel McGuire's disapproval.

Not until her most recent discussion with Samuel did Joy realize she completely misunderstood her father's warnings. He didn't dislike James, quite the contrary, in fact. The list he compiled, citing James's positive character traits, was lengthy indeed. No, the sole purpose of his admonition was to protect Joy from possible pain. But now, with James's complete recovery virtually assured, there was no longer any danger of his causing her grief.

She would tell him...today!

⌒

Joy was saving the dress for a special occasion. And what could be more special than accepting a marriage proposal from the man she loved? This time she would say yes!

Months ago, Samuel brought her several yards of gold and green plaid cotton, along with a length of black velvet ribbon. And when he returned from his last trip to Philadelphia, he brought a tattered issue of *Godey's Ladies Magazine*. Using one of the magazine pictures as a guide, Joy designed a gown—the snug waist and flared skirt flattering to her womanly contours. Four inch-wide strips of black velvet created wide V's across the bodice of the dress. To trim the dress, she cut the buttons from one of her mother's frocks, covered them with the black ribbon, and attached one at the outer edge of each V.

Then Joy braided her hair, as usual, gathering the braids in a bun on top of her head and securing them with the remaining black velvet. After adjusting her favorite wool shawl around her shoulders, Joy was ready for her meeting with James.

She borrowed Samuel's horse, filled a picnic basket with fried chicken, biscuits, bread-and-butter pickles, fresh-brewed tea, and cherry cobbler and headed north toward Plumtree Orchards.

As she made her way down the long, winding lane that joined the Sheffield plantation with the main road, Joy could see James busily repairing a fence post. Even from this distance, she sensed his masculine presence—muscles straining beneath the blue fabric of his collarless shirt, top three buttons undone to catch a breeze on this unseasonably warm December day. Wide black suspenders supported caramel-colored trousers, and his knee-high riding boots were caked with mud. Now and then, James used the back of his hand to push a strand of windblown hair from his eyes.

So absorbed was he with his work that he failed to hear the clip-clop of the horse's hooves. Joy grinned mischievously. Such intensity fit well into her plan.

When she had but fifty yards to go, Joy spurred her horse into a full gallop, reining it in when James straightened in response to the pounding hoofbeats. "Hello there!" she called merrily, sliding from her saddle to the ground and stripping off her riding gloves.

He smiled politely. "Joy…what brings you so far from town?"

"You do."

"I do?"

Nodding, she handed him the reins. "You look as though you could use some nourishment," she said, taking his hand and leading him down the drive. "I've made you a delicious lunch. And just wait 'til you see what's for dessert!"

She continued to chatter as they walked the rest of the way to the mansion. Inside, while James stepped out of sight to wash up, Joy quickly unfastened several of the buttons on her right boot. That done, she went into the kitchen, observing the less-than-tidy appearance of Missy's former domain. The place definitely needed a woman's touch, she decided. Then Joy set a proper table, pouring the tea into two, heavy mugs she found on a shelf above the cookstove.

When James returned, he seemed uncomfortable in her presence, but Joy shrugged it aside. As soon as she explained the real reason for her visit, he'd be his cheerful self again, she hoped. She watched him contentedly munch a drumstick, then butter a biscuit.

"Delicious," he admitted, still puzzled. "Is it my birthday?"

"I believe you said your birthday was sometime in August."

"So what is the occasion, then?"

Joy hesitated—the first time since arriving at his house. For a moment, she wondered if she possessed the courage to carry out her plan. But she cleared her throat, took a sip of the cool tea, and began....

Lifting a corner of her hem, she wiggled her foot. "Oh, dear," she said. "It seems my shoe buttons have come undone." Looking him in the eye, she added, "James, would you mind...?"

James's brow furrowed with confusion, but he got onto one knee, nonetheless, and attempted to fasten the tiny buttons. "If you don't stop squirming, I'll be here all afternoon," he complained good-naturedly.

She held out her hand. "Oh, my! I seem to have collected a splinter in my finger. Do you think you could remove it?"

The furrow on his brow deepened as he took her hand and inspected it. "I must say, Joy, that you're behaving mighty strangely today."

She ignored his scolding tone. It, too, would soon be gone—at least, she hoped so....

"You're right, of course. But as long as we're on the subject..."

His eyes, as he knelt before her, were almost on a level with hers. Joy wanted to caress the dear face so near her own. But there would be plenty of time for affectionate pats...later.

"What on earth are you talking about?" he wanted to know.

She had to act—now—before he grew weary of this game and got to his feet. That mustn't happen...not if Joy's plan were to be successful.

"James, not long ago you asked me a question...a very important question. I'm very much afraid," she said, squeezing the hand that held her own, "that I gave the wrong answer."

His dark brows drew together in puzzlement. Then, a faint smile tugged at the corners of his mouth. "At Drewry's wedding, you mean?"

Joy nodded. "Yes...just before the reception ended. You walked me to a weeping willow, sat me down on a boulder, and..."

Joy daintily laid her free hand upon her bosom and feigned total surprise. "Why, James! You were in this very position that day, too! Isn't that amazing?"

His beautiful smile was fully in place as he began to comprehend the trouble she took to recreate the scene. "Amazing," he echoed, winking. "Did I say something like 'Will you marry me, Joy?'"

She wrinkled her nose. "It was more like, 'Miss Naomi Joy McGuire, will you do me the honor of becoming my bride?' And you didn't say it out loud, you whispered it, softly."

James took a deep breath, his eyes twinkling. "Oh, I did, did I?"

"Yes, you did."

"Well, then, Miss Naomi Joy McGuire, will you..."

She threw her arms around his neck and kissed him soundly. "Yes! Oh, yes!" she squealed. "I thought you'd never ask!"

⌒

In the days that passed, James and Joy began making plans for their future together. They'd marry on the first Saturday in the spring—to combine the celebration of their new lives with the new life that would be bursting all around them.

They'd exchange their wedding vows at the altar at St. John's, with her father officiating. Jeb would be James's best man, and Running Deer, Joy's matron of honor. Joy already selected the material for her wedding gown; James made arrangements for their honeymoon at Richmond's grand Chesterfield Hotel.

They talked of children and grandchildren, of life at Plumtree Orchards, of continuing their work in the Suscataway village.

There would be long walks through the orchard after supper and long talks over coffee when breakfast was over. They'd attend services every Sunday, and afterward, Samuel and Jeb and Missy would join them for dinner.

They'd spend Christmas in Richmond with Drewry and Chase and their children, and every Fourth of July, the Auburns would travel north to watch the fireworks display above Fort McHenry with the Sheffield family.

The Sheffield family. The mere thought was exhilarating. From the moment he met Joy and began spending time with the Suscataway children, he knew God intended him to be a father. James loved the children's inquisitive minds, their cheerful outlook, their ability to see heaven on the cloudiest day. He and Joy would welcome and love any child God sent their way, whether Suscataway or Sheffield or stray.

Joy…

Like an angel, came to him from heaven during his darkest hour. And, like a guardian angel, she saved him from himself. James would spend the rest of his days giving humble thanks for this diminutive woman who made such a gigantic change in his life. She was his light, his love…his Joy

ABOUT THE AUTHOR

A prolific writer, Loree Lough has more than seventy books, sixty short stories, and 2,500 articles in print. Her stories have earned dozens of industry and Reader's Choice awards. A frequent guest speaker for writers' organizations, book clubs, private and government institutions, corporations, college and high school writing programs, and more, Loree has encouraged thousands with her comedic approach to "learned-the-hard-way" lessons about the craft and industry.

For decades, Loree has been an avid wolf enthusiast, and she dedicates a portion of her income each year to efforts that benefit the magnificent animals. She splits her time between a home in the Baltimore suburbs and a cabin in the Allegheny Mountains. She shares her life and residences with a spoiled pointer named Cash and her patient, dedicated husband, Larry, who has supported her writing and teaching endeavors throughout the years.

Loree loves hearing from her readers, so feel free to write her at loree@loreelough.com. To learn more about Loree and her books, visit her Web site at www.loreelough.com.